THE RESTLESS DEAD

THE RESTLESS DEAD

Ten Original Stories of the Supernatural

EDITED BY

DEBORAH NOYES

**WALKER
BOOKS**

These stories are works of fiction. Names, characters, places,
and incidents are either the product of the author's imagination or,
if real, are used fictitiously.

First published 2007 by Walker Books Ltd
87 Vauxhall Walk, London SE11 5HJ

2 4 6 8 10 9 7 5 3 1

Introduction © 2007 Deborah Noyes
Compilation © 2007 Deborah Noyes

Printed in the UK by CPI Bookmarque, Croydon, CR0 4TD

British Library Cataloguing in Publication Data:
a catalogue record for this book is available from the British Library

ISBN 978-1-4063-0968-3

www.walkerbooks.co.uk

For Clyde Wayshak

CONTENTS

INTRODUCTION   9

THE WRONG GRAVE   15
Kelly Link

THE HOUSE AND THE LOCKET   45
Chris Wooding

KISSING DEAD BOYS   65
Annette Curtis Klause

THE HEART OF ANOTHER   83
Marcus Sedgwick

THE NECROMANCERS   105
Herbie Brennan

NO VISIBLE POWER   123
Deborah Noyes

BAD THINGS   143
Libba Bray

THE GRAY BOY'S WORK   171
M. T. Anderson

THE POISON EATERS   209
Holly Black

HONEY IN THE WOUND   233
Nancy Etchemendy

ABOUT THE AUTHORS   261

Rest in peace.

It's our solemn wish, our plea for our dead.

The idea of death as eternal sleep is an old one, but almost as old are tales of the undead, those who won't or can't lie down and do what's expected of them.

Every culture has its strategies and safeguards for seeing the dead on their way. We hire professional wailing women to lament them, sprinkle them with herbs, lay coins on their eyelids. We fill their tombs with food and drink, riches, servants, pets, and painted boats, even life-size clay armies. We may then refuse to speak their names, but we honor and appease with flags and flowers, bake them cakes, picnic over their sleeping bones.

Even before a body dies, we tend the "loosening" soul. A "good" death, a peaceful one, is about readiness. So a Pima tribal elder might furnish the dying with owl feathers, a Catholic priest offer last rites, a Buddhist read aloud from the Tibetan Book of the Dead. If we don't prepare a vital, transitioning spirit, it departs unprotected. Or won't depart at all.

Whether the classic forlorn figure in white or a full-scale vision from another dimension—as in Chris Wooding's "The House and the Locket"—ghosts have unfinished business. Wrenched from familiar flesh, caught between matter and absence, they hang around, cautioning and blaming and wringing their useless hands, or, as in Libba Bray's "Bad Things," just reflecting the random nature of evil.

Vampires are a class of undead that feeds on the living, and in "Kissing Dead Boys," Annette Curtis Klause toys with the familiar dynamic of predator and prey.

In Holly Black's "The Poison Eaters," hunger for the flesh or essence of another promises not renewal but defeat.

The living in these tales, meanwhile, conduct their own dark affairs. Marcus Sedgwick's "The Heart of Another" summons the shade of Poe while illustrating the brutal lengths to which people go to *avoid* giving up the ghost.

In classic literature from Shelley's *Frankenstein* to Jacobs's "The Monkey's Paw" to King's *Pet Sematary*, worldly ambition or grief evoke a costly form of greed. Nancy Etchemendy's "Honey in the Wound" follows this tradition, while in Kelly Link's "The Wrong Grave" and Herbie Brennan's "The Necromancers," the resurrected dead blithely rebel in service of their own agendas.

Whether they are motivated by shock, sorrow, self-preservation, or more subtle ambitions—as in M.T. Anderson's richly allegorical "The Gray Boy's Work"—the dead in this anthology are all restless, all awake when they shouldn't be, all conspiring to keep *you* up at night.

Enjoy.

—Deborah Noyes

The Restless Dead

The Wrong Grave

Kelly Link

All of this happened because a boy I once knew named Miles Sperry decided to go into the resurrectionist business and dig up the grave of his girlfriend, Bethany Baldwin, who had been dead for not quite a year. Miles planned to do this in order to recover the sheaf of poems he had, in what he'd felt was a beautiful and romantic gesture, put into her casket. Or possibly it had just been a really dumb thing to do. He hadn't made copies. Miles had always been impulsive. I think you should know that right up front.

He'd tucked the poems, handwritten, tearstained, and with cross-outs, under Bethany's hands. Her fingers had felt like candles, fat and waxy and pleasantly cool, until you remembered that they were fingers. And he

couldn't help noticing that there was something wrong
about her breasts; they seemed larger. If Bethany had
known that she was going to die, would she have gone
all the way with him? One of his poems was about that,
about how now they never would, how it was too late
now. Carpe diem before you run out of diem.

Bethany's eyes were closed; someone had done that,
too, just like they'd arranged her hands, and even her
smile looked composed, in the wrong sense of the word.
Miles wasn't sure how you made someone smile after
they were dead. Bethany didn't look much like she had
when she'd been alive. That had been only a few days
ago. It was the nearest Miles had ever been to a dead
person, and he stood there, looking at Bethany, wishing
two things: that he were dead, too, and also that it had
seemed appropriate to bring along his notebook and a
pen. He felt he should be taking notes. After all, this
was the most significant thing that had ever happened
to Miles. A great change was occurring within him, moment by singular moment.

Poets were supposed to be in the moment and also
stand outside the moment, looking in. For example,
Miles had never noticed before, but Bethany's ears were
slightly lopsided. One was smaller and slightly higher
up. Not that he would have cared, or written a poem
about it or even mentioned it to her, ever, in case
it made her self-conscious, but it was a fact and now
that he'd noticed it, he thought it might have driven

him crazy, not mentioning it: he bent over and kissed Bethany's forehead, breathing in. She smelled like a new car. Miles's mind was full of poetic thoughts. Every cloud had a silver lining, except there was probably a more interesting and meaningful way to say that, and death wasn't really a cloud. He thought about what it was: more like an earthquake, maybe, or falling from a great height and smacking into the ground, really hard, which knocked the wind out of you and made it hard to sleep or wake up or eat or care about things like homework or whether there was anything good on TV. And death was foggy, too, but also prickly, so maybe instead of a cloud, a fog made of little sharp things. Needles. Every death fog has a lot of silver needles. Did that make sense? Did it scan?

Then the thought came to Miles, like the tolling of a large and leaden bell, that Bethany was dead. This may sound strange, but in my experience it's strange and it's also just how it works. You wake up and you remember that the person you love is dead. And then you think: *Really?*

Then you think how strange it is, how you have to remind yourself that the person you love is dead, and even while you're thinking about that, the thought comes to you again that the person you love is dead. And it's the same stupid fog, the same needles or mallet to the intestines or whatever worse thing you want to call it, all over again. But you'll see for yourself someday.

Miles stood there remembering, until Bethany's mother, Mrs. Baldwin, came up beside him. Her eyes were dry, but her hair was a mess. She'd only managed to put eyeshadow on one eyelid. She was wearing jeans and one of Bethany's old T-shirts. Not even one of Bethany's favorite T-shirts. Miles felt embarrassed for her, and for Bethany, too.

"What's that?" Mrs. Baldwin said. Her voice sounded rusty and outlandish, as if she were translating from some other language. Something Indo-Germanic, perhaps.

"My poems. Poems I wrote for her," Miles said. He felt very solemn. This was a historic moment. One day Miles's biographers would write about this. "Three haikus, a sestina, and two villanelles. Some longer pieces. No one else will ever read them."

Mrs. Baldwin looked into Miles's face with her terrible, dry eyes. "I see," she said. "She said you were a lousy poet." She put her hand down into the casket, smoothed Bethany's favorite dress, the one with spiderwebs and several holes through which you could see Bethany's itchy black tights. She patted Bethany's hands, and said, "Well, good-bye, old girl. Don't forget to send a postcard."

Don't ask me what she meant by this. Sometimes Bethany's mother said strange things. She was a lapsed Buddhist and a substitute math teacher. Once she'd caught Miles cheating on an algebra quiz. Relations between Miles and Mrs. Baldwin had not improved during the time that Bethany and Miles were dating, and Miles couldn't decide whether or not to believe her about Bethany not liking his poetry. Substitute teachers had strange senses of humor when they had them at all.

He almost reached into the casket and took his poetry back. But Mrs. Baldwin would have thought that she'd proved something; that she'd won. Not that this was a situation where anyone was going to win anything. This was a funeral, not a game show. Nobody was going to get to take Bethany home.

Mrs. Baldwin looked at Miles and Miles looked back. Bethany wasn't looking at anyone. The two people that Bethany had loved most in the world could see, through that dull hateful fog, what the other was thinking, just for a minute, and although you weren't there, and even if you had been, you wouldn't have known what they were thinking anyway, I'll tell you. *I wish it had been me*, Miles thought. And Mrs. Baldwin thought, *I wish it had been you, too.*

Miles put his hands into the pockets of his new suit, turned, and left Mrs. Baldwin standing there. He went and sat next to his own mother, who was trying very hard not to cry. She'd liked Bethany. Everyone had liked Bethany. A few rows in front, a girl named April Lamb was picking her nose in some kind of frenzy of grief. When they got to the cemetery, there was another funeral service going on, the burial of the girl who had been in the other car, and the two groups of mourners glared at each other as they parked their cars and tried to figure out which grave to gather around.

Two florists had misspelled Bethany's name on the ugly wreaths, BERTHANY and also BETHONY, just like tribe members did when they were voting each other out on the television show *Survivor*, which had always been Bethany's favorite thing about *Survivor*. Bethany had been an excellent speller, although the Lutheran minister who was conducting the sermon didn't mention that.

Miles had an uncomfortable feeling: he became aware that he couldn't wait to get home and call Bethany, to tell her all about this, about everything that had happened since she'd died. He sat and waited until the feeling wore off. It was a feeling he was getting used to.

Bethany had liked Miles because he made her laugh. He makes me laugh, too. Miles figured that digging up Bethany's grave, even that would have made her laugh. Bethany had had a great laugh, which went up and up like a clarinetist on an escalator. It wasn't annoying. It had been delightful, if you liked that kind of laugh. It would have made Bethany laugh that Miles Googled "grave digging" in order to educate himself. He read an Edgar Allan Poe story, he watched several relevant episodes of *Buffy the Vampire Slayer*, and he bought Vicks VapoRub, which you were supposed to apply under your nose. He bought equipment at Target: a special, battery-operated, telescoping shovel; a set of wire cutters; a flashlight; extra batteries for the shovel and flashlight; and even a Velcro headband with a headlamp that came with a special red lens filter, so that you were less likely to be noticed.

Miles printed out a map of the cemetery so that he could find his way to Bethany's grave off Weeping Fish Lane, even—as an acquaintance of mine once remarked— "in the dead of night when naught can be seen, so pitch is the dark." (Not that the dark would be very pitch. Miles had picked a night when the moon would be full.) The map was also just in case, because he'd seen movies where the dead rose from their graves. You wanted to have all the exits marked in a situation like that.

He told his mother that he was spending the night at his friend John's house. He told his friend John not to tell his mother anything.

If Miles had Googled "poetry" as well as "digging up graves," he would have discovered that his situation was not without precedent. The poet and painter Dante Gabriel Rossetti also buried his poetry with his dead lover. Rossetti, too, had regretted this gesture, had eventually decided to dig up his lover to get back his poems. I'm telling you this so that you never make the same mistake.

I can't tell you whether Dante Gabriel Rossetti was a better poet than Miles, although Rossetti had a sister, Christina Rossetti, who was really something. But you're not interested in my views on poetry. I know you better than that, even if you don't know me. You're waiting for me to get to the part about grave digging.

Miles had a couple of friends and he thought about asking someone to come along on the expedition. But no one except for Bethany knew that Miles wrote poetry. And Bethany had been dead for a while. Eleven months, in fact, which was one month longer than Bethany had been Miles's girlfriend. Long enough that Miles was beginning to make his way out of the fog and the needles. Long enough that he could listen to certain songs on the radio again. Long enough that sometimes there was something dreamlike about his memories of Bethany, as if she'd been a movie that he'd seen a long time ago, late at night on television. Long enough that when he tried to reconstruct the poems he'd written her, especially the villanelle, which had been, in his opinion, really quite good, he couldn't. It was as if when he'd put those poems into the casket, he hadn't just given Bethany the only copies of some poems but had instead given away those shining, perfect lines, given them away so thoroughly that he'd never be able to write them out again. Miles knew that Bethany was dead. There was nothing to do about that. But the poetry was different. You have to salvage what you can, even if you're the one who buried it in the first place.

* * *

You might think at certain points in this story that I'm being hard on Miles, that I'm not sympathetic to his situation. This isn't true. I'm as fond of Miles as I am of anyone else. I don't think he's any stupider or any bit less special or remarkable than—for example—you. Anyone might accidentally dig up the wrong grave. It's a mistake anyone could make.

The moon was full, and the map was easy to read even without the aid of the flashlight. The cemetery was full of cats. Don't ask me why. Miles was not afraid. He was resolute. The battery-operated telescoping shovel at first refused to untelescope. He'd tested it in his own backyard, but here, in the cemetery, it seemed unbearably loud. It scared off the cats for a while, but it didn't draw any unwelcome attention. The cats came back. Miles set aside the wreaths and bouquets, and then he used his wire cutters to trace a rectangle. He stuck the telescoping shovel under and pried up fat squares of sod above Bethany's grave. He stacked them up like carpet samples and got to work.

By two AM, Miles had knotted a length of rope at short, regular intervals for footholds and then looped it around a tree so he'd be able to climb out of the grave again once he'd retrieved his poetry. He was waist-deep in the hole he'd made. The night was warm, and he was sweating. It was hard work, directing the shovel. Every once in a while it telescoped while he was using it. He'd borrowed his mother's gardening gloves to keep from getting blisters, but still his hands were getting tired. The gloves were too big. His arms ached.

By three thirty, Miles could no longer see out of the grave in any direction except up. A large white cat came and peered down at Miles, grew bored, and left again. The moon moved over Miles's head like a spotlight. He began to wield the shovel more carefully. He didn't want to damage Bethany's casket. When the shovel struck something that was not dirt, Miles remembered that he'd left the Vicks VapoRub on his bed at home. He improvised with a cherry Chap Stick he found in his pocket. Now he used his garden-gloved hands to dig and to smooth dirt away. The bloody light emanating from his Velcro headband picked out the ingenious telescoping ridges of the discarded shovel, the little rocks and worms and wormlike roots that poked out of the dirt walls of Miles's excavation, the lid of Bethany's casket.

Miles realized he was standing on the lid. Perhaps he should have made the hole a bit wider. It would be difficult to get the lid open while standing on it. He needed to pee: there was that as well. So he pulled himself back up along the rope with his tired, tired hands and went off to find somewhere private. When he came back, he shone his flashlight into the grave. It seemed to him that the lid of the coffin was slightly ajar. Was that possible? Had he damaged the hinges with the telescoping shovel or kicked the lid askew somehow when he was shimmying up the rope? He essayed a slow, judicious sniff, but all he smelled was dirt and cherry Chap Stick. He applied more cherry Chap Stick, just in case. Then he lowered himself into the grave.

The lid wobbled when he tested it with his feet. He decided that if he kept hold of the rope and slid his foot down and under the lid, like so, then perhaps he could cantilever the lid up—

It was very strange. It felt as if something had hold of his foot. He tried to tug it free, but no: his foot was stuck, caught in some kind of vise or grip. He lowered the toe of his other hiking boot down into the black gap between the coffin and its lid and tentatively poked it forward, but this produced no result. He'd have to let go of the rope and lift the lid with his hands. Balance like so, carefully, carefully, on the thin rim of the casket. Figure out how he was caught.

It was hard work, balancing and lifting at the same time, although the one foot was still firmly wedged in its accidental toehold. Miles became aware of his own breathing, the furtive scuffling noise of his other boot against the coffin lid. Even the red beam of his lamp as it pitched and swung, back and forth, up and down, in the narrow space seemed unutterably noisy. "Shit, shit, shit," Miles whispered. It was either that or else scream. He got his fingers under the lid of the coffin on either side of his feet and bent his wobbly knees so he wouldn't hurt his back lifting. Something touched the fingers of his right hand.

No, his fingers had touched something. *Don't be ridiculous, Miles.* He yanked the lid up as fast and hard as he could, the way you would rip off a bandage if you suspected there were baby spiders hatching under it. "Shit, shit, shit, shit, shit!"

He yanked and someone else pushed. The lid shot up and fell back against the opposite embankment of dirt. The dead girl who had hold of Miles's boot let go.

This was the first of the many unexpected and unpleasant shocks that Miles was to endure for the sake of poetry. The second was the sickening—no, shocking— shock that he had dug up the wrong grave, the wrong dead girl.

The wrong dead girl was lying there, smiling up at him, and her eyes were open. She was several years older than Bethany. She was taller and had a significantly more developed rack. She even had a tattoo.

The smile of the wrong dead girl was white and orthodontically perfected. Bethany had had braces that turned kissing into a heroic feat. You had to kiss around braces, slide your tongue up or sideways or under, like navigating through barbed wire: a delicious, tricky trip through no-man's-land. Bethany pursed her mouth forward when she kissed. If Miles forgot and mashed his lips down too hard on hers, she whacked him on the back of his head. This was one of the things about his relationship with Bethany that Miles remembered vividly as he looked down at the wrong dead girl.

The wrong dead girl spoke first. "Knock knock," she said.

"What?" Miles said.

"Knock knock," the wrong dead girl said again.

"Who's there?" Miles said.

"Gloria," the wrong dead girl said. "Gloria Palnick. Who are you and what are you doing in my grave?"

"This isn't your grave," Miles said, aware that he was arguing with a dead girl, and the wrong dead girl at that. "This is Bethany's grave. What are you doing in Bethany's grave?"

"Oh no," Gloria Palnick said. "This is my grave and I get to ask the questions."

A notion crept, like little dead cat feet, over Miles. Possibly he had made a dangerous and deeply embarrassing mistake. "Poetry," he managed to say. "There was some poetry that I, ah, that I accidentally left in my girl-friend's casket. And there's a deadline for a poetry contest coming up, and so I really, really needed to get it back."

The dead girl stared at him. There was something about her hair that Miles didn't like.

"Excuse me, but are you for real?" she said. "This sounds like one of those lame excuses. The dog ate my homework. I accidentally buried my poetry with my dead girlfriend."

"Look," Miles said, "I checked the tombstone and everything. This is supposed to be Bethany's grave. Bethany Baldwin. I'm really sorry I bothered you and everything, but this isn't really my fault." The dead girl just stared at him thoughtfully. He wished that she would blink. She wasn't smiling anymore. Her hair, lank and black, where Bethany's had been brownish and frizzy in summer, was writhing a little, like snakes. Miles thought of centipedes. Inky midnight tentacles.

"Maybe I should just go away," Miles said. "Leave you to, ah, rest in peace or whatever."

"I don't think 'sorry' cuts the mustard here," Gloria Palnick said. She barely moved her mouth when she spoke, Miles noticed dreamily. And yet her enunciation was fine. "Besides, I'm sick of this place. It's boring. Maybe I'll just come along with you."

"What?" Miles said. He felt behind himself, surreptitiously, for the knotted rope.

"I said, maybe I'll come with," Gloria Palnick said. She sat up. Her hair was really coiling around, really seething now. Miles thought he could hear hissing noises.

"You can't do that!" he said. "I'm sorry, but no. Just no."

"Well then, you stay here and keep me company," Gloria Palnick said. Her hair was really something.

"I can't do that, either," Miles said, trying to explain quickly, before the dead girl's hair decided to strangle him. "I'm going to be a poet. It would be a great loss to the world if I never got a chance to publish my poetry."

"I see," Gloria Palnick said, as if she did, in fact, see a great deal. Her hair settled back down on her shoulders and began to act a lot more like hair. "You don't want me to come home with you. You don't want to stay here with me. Then how about this? If you're such a great poet, then write me a poem. Write something about me so that everyone will be sad that I died."

"I could do that," Miles said. Relief bubbled up through his middle like tiny donuts bobbing in an industrial deep-fat fryer. "Let's do that. You lie down and make yourself comfortable and I'll rebury you. Today I've got a quiz in American history, and I was going to study for it during my free period after lunch, but I could write a poem for you instead."

"Today is Saturday," the dead girl said.

"Oh, hey," Miles said. "Then no problem. I'll go straight home and work on your poem. Should be done by Monday."

"Not so fast," Gloria Palnick said. "You need to know all about my life and about me if you're going to write a poem about me, right? And how do I know you'll write a poem if I let you bury me again? How will I know if the poem's any good? No dice. I'm coming home with you and I'm sticking around until I get my poem, 'kay?"

She stood up. She was several inches taller than Miles. "Do you have any Chap Stick?" she said. "My lips are really dry."

"Here," Miles said. Then, "You can keep it."

"Oh, afraid of dead-girl cooties," Gloria Palnick said. She smacked her lips at him in an upsetting way.

"I'll climb up first," Miles said. He had the idea that if he could just get up the rope, if he could yank the rope up after himself fast enough, he might be able to run away, get to the fence where he'd chained up his bike, before Gloria managed to get out. It wasn't like she knew where he lived. She didn't even know his name.

"Fine," Gloria said. She looked like she knew what Miles was thinking and didn't really care. By the time Miles had bolted up the rope, yanking it up out of the grave, abandoning the telescoping shovel, the wire cutters, the wronged dead girl, and had unlocked his road bike and was racing down the empty 5:00 AM road, the little red dot of light from his headlamp falling into potholes, he'd almost managed to persuade himself that it had all been a grisly hallucination. Except for the fact that the dead girl's cold dead arms were around his waist, suddenly, and her cold dead face was pressed against his back, her damp hair coiling around his head and tapping at his mouth, burrowing down his filthy shirt.

"Don't leave me like that again," she said.

"No," Miles said. "I won't. Sorry."

He couldn't take the dead girl home. He couldn't think of how to explain it to his parents. No, no, no. He didn't want to take her over to John's house, either. It was far too complicated. Not just the girl, but he was covered in dirt. John wouldn't be able to keep his big mouth shut.

"Where are we going?" the dead girl said.

"I know a place," Miles said. "Could you please not put your hands under my shirt? They're really cold. And your fingernails are kind of sharp."

"Sorry," the dead girl said.

They rode along in silence until they were passing the 7-Eleven at the corner of Eighth and Walnut, and the dead girl said, "Could we stop for a minute? I'd like some beef jerky. And a diet Coke."

Miles braked. "Beef jerky?" he said. "Is that what dead people eat?"

"It's the preservatives," the dead girl said, somewhat obscurely.

Miles gave up. He steered the bike into the parking lot. "Let go, please," he said. The dead girl let go. He got off the bike and turned around. He'd been wondering just exactly how she'd managed to sit behind him on the bike, and he saw that she was sitting above the rear tire on a cushion of her horrible, shiny hair. Her legs were stretched out on either side, toes in black combat boots floating just above the asphalt, and yet the bike didn't fall over. It just hung there under her. For the first time in almost a month, Miles found himself thinking about Bethany as if she were still alive: Bethany is never going to believe this. But then, Bethany had never believed in anything like ghosts. She'd hardly believed in the school dress code. She definitely wouldn't have believed in a dead girl who could float around on her hair like it was an antigravity device.

"I can also speak fluent Spanish," Gloria Palnick said.

Miles reached into his back pocket for his wallet and discovered that the pocket was full of dirt. "I can't go in there," he said. "For one thing, I'm a kid and it's five in the morning. Also I look like I just escaped from a gang of naked mole rats. I'm filthy."

The dead girl just looked at him. He said coaxingly, "*You* should go in. You're older. I'll give you all the money I've got. You go in and I'll stay out here and work on the poem."

"You'll ride off and leave me here," the dead girl said. She didn't sound angry, just matter of fact. But her hair was beginning to float up. It lifted her up off Miles's bike in a kind of hairy cloud and then plaited itself down her back in a long businesslike rope.

"I won't," Miles promised. "Here. Take this. Buy whatever you want."

Gloria Palnick took the money. "How very generous of you," she said.

"No problem," Miles told her. "I'll wait here." And he did wait. He waited until Gloria Palnick went into the 7-Eleven. Then he counted to thirty, waited one second more, got back on his bike, and rode away. By the time he'd made it to the meditation cabin in the woods back behind Bethany's mother's house, where he and Bethany had liked to sit and play Monopoly, Miles felt as if things were under control again, more or less. There is nothing so calming as a meditation cabin where long, boring games of Monopoly have taken place. He'd clean up in the cabin sink and maybe take a nap. Bethany's mother never went out there. Her ex-husband's meditation clothes, his scratchy prayer mat, all his Buddhas and scrolls and incense holders and posters of Che Guevara were still out here. Miles had snuck into the cabin a few times since Bethany's death, to sit in the dark and listen to the plink-plink of the meditation fountain and think about things. He was sure Bethany's mother wouldn't have minded if she knew, although he hadn't ever asked, just in case. Which had been wise of him.

The key to the cabin was on the beam just above the door, but he didn't need it after all. The door stood open. There was a smell of incense and of other things: cherry Chap Stick and dirt and beef jerky. There was a pair of black combat boots beside the door.

Miles squared his shoulders. I have to admit that he was behaving sensibly here, finally. Finally. Because— and Miles and I are in agreement for once—if the dead girl could follow him somewhere before he even knew exactly where he was going, then there was no point in running away. Anywhere he went, she'd already be there. Miles took off his shoes, because you were supposed to take off your shoes when you went into the cabin. It was a gesture of respect. He put them down beside the combat boots and went inside. The waxed pine floor felt silky under his bare feet. He looked down and saw that he was walking on Gloria Palnick's hair.

"Sorry!" Miles said. He meant several things by that. He meant sorry for walking on your hair. Sorry for riding off and leaving you in the 7-Eleven after promising that I wouldn't. Sorry for the grave wrong I've done you. But most of all he meant sorry, dead girl, that I ever dug you up in the first place.

"Don't mention it," the dead girl said. "Want some jerky?"

Miles became aware that he was hungry. "Sure," he said.

He was beginning to feel he would have liked this dead girl under other circumstances, despite her annoying, bullying hair. She had poise. A sense of humor. She seemed to have what his mother called stick-to-itiveness, what the AP English Exam prefers to call tenacity. Miles recognized the quality. He had it in no small degree himself. The dead girl was also extremely pretty, if you ignored the hair. You might think less of Miles that he thought so well of the dead girl, that this was a betrayal of Bethany. *Miles* felt it was a betrayal. But he thought that Bethany might have liked the dead girl, too. She would certainly have liked her tattoo.

"How is the poem coming?" the dead girl said.

"There's not a lot that rhymes with Gloria," Miles said. "Or Palnick."

"Toothpick," said the dead girl. There was a fragment of jerky caught in her teeth. "Euphoria."

"Maybe *you* should write the stupid poem," Miles said. There was an awkward pause, broken only by the almost-noiseless glide of hair retreating across a pine floor. Miles sat down, sweeping the floor with his hand, just in case.

"You were going to tell me something about your life," he said.

"Boring," Gloria Palnick said. "Short. Over."

"That's not much to work with. Unless you want a haiku."

"Tell me about this girl you were trying to dig up," Gloria said. "The one you wrote the poetry for."

"Her name was Bethany," Miles said. "She died in a car crash."

"Was she pretty?" Gloria said.

"Yeah," Miles said.

"You liked her a lot," Gloria said.

"Yeah," Miles said.

"Are you sure you're a poet?" Gloria asked.

Miles was silent. He gnawed his jerky ferociously. It tasted like dirt. Maybe he'd write a poem about it. That would show Gloria Palnick.

He swallowed and said, "Why were you in Bethany's grave?"

"How should I know?" she said. She was sitting across from him, leaning against a concrete Buddha the size of a three-year-old, but much fatter and holier. Her hair hung down over her face, just like in a Japanese horror movie. "What do you think, that Bethany and I swapped coffins, just for fun?"

"Is Bethany like you?" Miles said. "Does she have weird hair and follow people around and scare them just for fun?"

"No," the dead girl said through her hair. "Not for fun. But what's wrong with having a little fun? It gets dull. And why should we stop having fun just because we're dead? It's not all demon cocktails and Scrabble down in the old bardo, you know?"

"You know what's weird?" Miles said. "You sound like her. Bethany. You say the same kind of stuff."

"It was dumb to try to get your poems back," said the dead girl. "You can't just give something to somebody and then take it back again."

"I just miss her," Miles said. He began to cry.

After a while, the dead girl got up and came over to him. She took a big handful of her hair and wiped his face with it. It was soft and absorbent, and it made Miles's skin crawl. He stopped crying, which might have been what the dead girl was hoping. "Go home," she said.

Miles shook his head. "No," he finally managed to say. He was shivering like crazy.

"Why not?" the dead girl said.

"Because I'll go home and then you'll be there, waiting for me. And you'll eat my parents or tell them about how I dug up Bethany's grave. About how I couldn't even get that right."

"I won't," the dead girl said. "I promise."

"Really?" Miles said.

"I really promise," said the dead girl. "I'm sorry I teased you, Miles."

"That's okay," Miles said. He got up and then he just stood there, looking down at her. He seemed to be about to ask her something, and then he changed his mind. She could see this happen, and she could see why, too. He knew he ought to leave now, while she was willing to let him go. He didn't want to mess up by asking something impossible and obvious and stupid. That was okay by her. She couldn't be sure that he wouldn't say something that would rile up her hair. Not to mention the tattoo. She didn't think he'd noticed when her tattoo had started getting annoyed.

"Good-bye," Miles said at last. It almost looked as if he wanted her to shake his hand, but when she sent out a length of her hair, he turned and ran. It was a little disappointing. And the dead girl couldn't help but notice that he'd left his shoes and his bike behind.

The dead girl walked around the cabin, picking things up and putting them down again. She kicked the Monopoly box, which was a game that she'd always hated. That was one of the okay things about being dead, that nobody ever wanted to play Monopoly.

At last she came to the statue of Saint Francis, whose head had been knocked right off during an indoor game of croquet a long time ago. Bethany Baldwin had made

Saint Francis a lumpy substitute Ganesh head out of modeling clay. You could lift that clay elephant head off and there was a hollow space where Miles and Bethany had left secret things for each other. The dead girl reached down her shirt and into the cavity where her more interesting and useful organs had once been (she had been an organ donor). She'd kept Miles's poetry in there for safekeeping.

She folded up the poetry, wedged it inside Saint Francis, and fixed the Ganesh head back on. Maybe Miles would find it someday. She would have liked to see the look on his face.

We don't often get a chance to see our dead. Still less often do we know them when we see them. Mrs. Baldwin's eyes opened. She looked up and saw the dead girl and smiled. She said, "Bethany."

Bethany sat down on her mother's bed. She took her mother's hand. If Mrs. Baldwin thought Bethany's hand was cold, she didn't say so. She held on tightly. "I was dreaming about you," she told Bethany. "You were in an Andrew Lloyd Webber musical."

"It was just a dream," Bethany said.

Mrs. Baldwin reached up and touched a piece of Bethany's hair with her other hand. "You've changed your hair," she said. "I like it."

They were both silent. Bethany's hair stayed very still. Perhaps it felt flattered.

"Thank you for coming back," Mrs. Baldwin said at last.

"I can't stay," Bethany said.

Mrs. Baldwin held her daughter's hand tighter. "I'll go with you. That's why you've come, isn't it? Because I'm dead, too?"

Bethany shook her head. "No. Sorry. You're not dead. It's Miles's fault. He dug me up."

"He did what?" Mrs. Baldwin said. She forgot the small, lowering unhappiness of discovering that she was not dead after all.

"He wanted his poetry back," Bethany said. "The poems he gave me."

"That idiot," Mrs. Baldwin said. It was exactly the sort of thing she expected of Miles, but only with the advantage of hindsight, because how could you really expect such a thing? "What did you do to him?"

"I played a good joke on him," Bethany said. She'd never really tried to explain her relationship with Miles to her mother. It seemed especially pointless now. She wriggled her fingers, and her mother instantly let go of Bethany's hand.

Being a former Buddhist, Mrs. Baldwin had always understood that when you hold on to your children too tightly, you end up pushing them away instead. Except that after Bethany had died, she wished she'd held on a little tighter. She drank up Bethany with her eyes. She noted the tattoo on Bethany's forearm with both

disapproval and delight. Disapproval, because one day
Bethany might regret getting a tattoo of a cobra that
wrapped all the way around her bicep. Delight, because
something about the tattoo suggested Bethany was
really here. That this wasn't just a dream. She would
never have dreamed that her daughter was alive again
and tattooed and wearing long, writhing, midnight tails
of hair.

"I have to go," Bethany said. She had turned her
head a little, toward the window as if she were listening
for something far away.

"Oh," her mother said, trying to sound as if she
didn't mind. She didn't want to ask: will you come
back? She was a lapsed Buddhist, but not so very lapsed,
after all. She was still working to relinquish all desire,
all hope, all self. When a person like Mrs. Baldwin suddenly finds that her life has been dismantled by a great
catastrophe, she may then hold on to her belief as if to a
life raft, even if the belief is this: that one should hold
on to nothing. Mrs. Baldwin had taken her Buddhism
very seriously once, before substitute teaching had
knocked it out of her.

Bethany stood up. "I'm sorry I wrecked the car," she
said, although this wasn't completely true. If she'd still
been alive, she would have been sorry. But she was
dead. She didn't know how to be sorry anymore. And
the longer she stayed, the more likely it seemed that her
hair would do something truly terrible. Her hair was

not good Buddhist hair. It did not love the living world or the things in the living world, and it *did not love* them in an utterly unenlightened way. There was nothing of light or enlightenment about Bethany's hair. It knew nothing of hope, but it had desires and ambitions. It's best not to speak of those ambitions. As for the tattoo, it wanted to be left alone. And to be allowed to eat people, just every once in a while.

When Bethany stood up, Mrs. Baldwin said suddenly, "I've been thinking I might give up substitute teaching."

Bethany waited.

"I might go to Japan to teach English," Mrs. Baldwin said. "Sell the house, just pack up and go. Is that okay with you? Do you mind?"

Bethany didn't mind. She bent over and kissed her mother on her forehead. She left a smear of cherry Chap Stick. When she had gone, Mrs. Baldwin got up and put on her bathrobe, the one with white cranes and frogs. She went downstairs and made coffee and sat at the kitchen table for a long time, staring at nothing. Her coffee got cold and she never even noticed.

The dead girl left town as the sun was coming up. I won't tell you where she went. Maybe she joined the circus and took part in daring trapeze acts that put her hair to good use, kept it from getting bored and plotting the destruction of all that is good and pure and lovely. Maybe she shaved her head and went on a pilgrimage to some remote lamasery and came back as a superhero with a dark past and some kick-ass martial-arts moves. Maybe she sent her mother postcards from time to time. Maybe she wrote them as part of her circus act, using the tips of her hair, dipping them into an inkwell. These postcards, not to mention her calligraphic scrolls, are highly sought after by collectors nowadays. I have two.

Miles stopped writing poetry for several years. He never went back to get his bike. He stayed away from graveyards and also from girls with long hair. The last I heard, he had a job writing topical haikus for the Weather Channel. One of his best-known haikus is the one about tropical storm Suzy. It goes something like this:

A young girl passes
in a hurry. Hair uncombed.
Full of black devils.

The House
and the Locket

Chris Wooding

I was, in my youth, a rogue. The Lord God blessed me with a handsome countenance, a pleasing posture, and an artful tongue with which to charm the fairer sex. I considered it sinful to waste such gifts in chastity.

Yet though I wandered often, there was one to whom I would always return. Her name was Lizabeth. She was clean and pure as a winter sun; and I loved her deeply, as she loved me.

Lizabeth became my companion at the age of six. Her mother had died in childbirth, and her father had fallen to consumption, poisoned by the black air of London. My family—whom, I understand, owed a great debt of friendship to her parents—took her away from the city and adopted her as a ward. And so we were as brother and sister, sharing the trials and joys of growing up.

When she reached ten years of age, she was sent to a boarding school, wherein she might learn the ways of a lady. I, meanwhile, learned the ways of men in the six years she was gone from me, and upon her return I looked at her with new eyes. For she was no longer the girl whom I had played childish games with: now she was quiet and thoughtful and full of secrets, and the games we played were entirely different.

In the fullness of time, passion bloomed between us, and we began courting. There was a stillness about Lizabeth that quieted the torment of adolescence, a calm center to my storm. But try as I might, I could not stay faithful to her. For days at a time I would be gone, into the city, exploring the rotten heart of the capital. I haunted the gin-palaces of Whitechapel while the Ripper stalked the shadows. I lounged in bars on the Strand in the company of certain ladies. I raked the underbelly of London and lapped at its wounds.

And always, when I returned, Lizabeth was waiting, patient and gentle. She would not scold me nor ask where I had been. Her acceptance shamed me more than any shrill words could have.

She spoke of it only once, not looking up from her embroidery. "You can wander," she said. "It is in you to wander. But in time that shall end, and you will return to me. You are mine, whether you know it or no."

I confess a shiver passed through me then. It was the certainty in her voice, the easy assuredness of her tone.

I know not what they taught her during those years in which we were apart, but it had made her fascinating and alien.

The next day, she gave me a locket.

I had a companion in my sordid endeavours, a young man who shared my hot blood. He, too, was the son of a wealthy family, and was fortunate enough to receive an income from his parents with which to indulge himself. His name was Henry, and it was to him that I went directly with the most dreadful news that I, at the age of eighteen, was to be married to Lizabeth.

"A tragedy indeed," he agreed. "You are to be cut down in the prime of your life."

We had retired to a public house where we were well-known. It seemed the correct thing to do, given the circumstances. I was gazing glumly at my locket, in which was the likeness of my sweetheart. Her blond curls still enchanted me, her eyes bewitched, and yet a shadow now lay on my heart and seemed to muffle it.

"I love her," I said. "Truly I love her."

"But do you love her enough? Enough to forbear all others, in the sight of God?" He drank deep from his mug and wiped the foam from his lips. "Just to think of it brings on the ague in me."

"It is my father's will. He believes a man must do the honorable thing. And he threatened to cut off my allowance if I do not propose within the month."

"Grotesque!" Henry declared. "Abominable! What horrors parents visit upon their children in the name of honor." He became sly. "But fear not, my friend. A married man may still visit the city, if business should take him there."

It was night when we left, and we pulled our greatcoats tight about us. Henry's abode—where I was to stay—was on the far side of a low hill, upon which lay a dense forest cut through with cart trails. We, being young men then and full of the invincibility of youth, thought nothing of the dark walk from manor to inn and back again. We feared neither robbers nor wolves, and besides, Henry carried a pistol to take care of either. Yet this night I was filled with a strange foreboding. A fog lurked in the hollows, and there was a chill in the air that slipped into the marrow.

"It is cold," I said. "Perhaps we should summon a cab and take the road around the hill?"

"Nonsense!" Henry cried. "Why, you already sound like a married man."

That was too much for me. Stoutly, I followed him as he marched away.

But my friend's bravado did little to dispel the sense that something was amiss. We had not gone very far when the fog began to thicken, bunching to cloud our sight. I had to hurry to keep up with him or else he would have faded into a ghostly shadow and left me alone in that place. I feared my courage would not stand that. He was whistling merrily, but I sensed that his cheerfulness was forced, and that even he was a little worried.

I did my best not to notice the sound of padding steps following us, dampened by the turf of the forest. Henry did the same.

"Are we nearly home, do you think?" I asked at one point, to which Henry replied, "I'm sure we are."

I was used to hearing Henry lie. It happened whenever he spoke to a woman. He was lying now. His hand never strayed far from where the pistol lay beneath his greatcoat.

The fog gathered still further, until it seemed that our world had closed around us. A damp gray emptiness lay beyond the limits of our vision. Black skeletons of trees approached in procession as we walked, then slid past and away, swallowed once more by the mist. We heard the sounds of sniffing behind us, and the intermittent tread of a beast, and then a strange, crooning mewl.

"A wolf," Henry muttered. "It will run if I fire my pistol. Don't worry, my friend."

But I was worried, because my instincts told me that whatever tracked us through the mist, it was no wolf.

We quickened our step, but the thing kept pace. We walked with hunched shoulders. Neither of us spoke of it, though our ears strained for the slightest sound. The beast seemed ever close, for we heard the scratch and tap of claws and the crack of twigs. Yet we caught no glimpse beyond what our fevered imaginations provided.

Then, from behind us, the beast *cackled*, a malevolent chuckle like that of an old hag. We had kept hold of our fear as long as we could, but when we heard that dreadful sound, our nerve failed us. We ran headlong into the mist, heedless of the lashing branches that hung in our path, seeking only to escape the horror at our backs. I fought to stay close to Henry, terrified that I should lose him in the murk. For a time, there was only the rushing of air, the beating of hearts, the gasp of breath, the crunch and whisper of the forest. When finally we could run no more, we came to a stop together, our chests heaving.

It was then that we saw the house.

God, I wish that we had never entered that place. If I had known then what I know now, I would have turned and taken my chances with the beast that had herded us there. But all we saw was a sanctuary, and we ran toward it.

It was ancient, a squat and imposing block of stone, surrounded by thick forest. Its edges were crumbling and its windows grimed. It seemed to grow as I looked upon it, as if swollen with the effort of containing something within. Its aspect made me fearful, but not so fearful as what hid in the fog, snuffling and chuckling at our heels. I hesitated for the briefest moment, warned against this place by some sense I could not identify, but Henry was already away toward the door. I followed.

The door was unlocked. Henry did not trouble to knock. We threw ourselves inside and secured the bolts behind us.

We listened for a time as our pursuer sniffed around the door and scratched at the jamb. Later, after we imagined it had given up, we heard a tapping at one of the downstairs windows, but neither of us dared look. We stood there in the hallway for a long time, until all sound had ceased.

We were left in the silence of the house.

It was dusty but not neglected. We listened, but there was no movement. The air smelled stale and was heavy with the chill of the fog. The rooms felt empty.

"Do you think it has gone?" I whispered.

"I think so," Henry replied.

"Should we look?"

Henry peered down the shadowy hallway. At the end were stairs, leading upward, and along its length were several doors, all open.

"Perhaps we should beg the indulgence of this house's owners for the night," he suggested.

"If, indeed, they are here," I replied.

"Hello?" cried Henry, at which there was the most unholy shriek from without and a furious assault on the door. We shied away in terror. The beast had been lurking outside, listening for us.

We fled up the stairs and hid on the landing. At any moment we expected the door to fly open and our pursuer to pounce through. The din was extraordinary, echoing through the vacant rooms of the manor.

But the door held.

When silence fell again, we were both shuddering. Henry looked at me and managed a sickly smile.

"Perhaps we should stay the night," he said.

I heartily agreed. The thing was out there somewhere, waiting for us. Perhaps it was prowling around the house even now, looking for a way in.

We searched the upper floor, finding nothing but empty rooms there. The house bore an air of temporary abandonment, but it had not been deserted. In the cupboards hung clothes, elegant dresses for a woman and dashing finery for a man. In a whimsical moment, I held a brocaded jacket up against me and found it a perfect fit. The owner's taste in clothes was impeccable. I would tell him so, if we should meet.

Henry pointed out a child's playroom, where toys were scattered. I found myself curious about the owners of this place and what had befallen them. If they were away, surely they would employ maids to tend to the house? And why was the door unlocked? Here and there we found pictures knocked askew, books lying open on the floor. All signs pointed to a hurried departure or some kind of upset. There was a large stain on the carpet of the upstairs landing, but the house was too dark to determine its nature. We dared not kindle the lamps, for fear that their glow would draw the creature, so we hunted without light.

We found no pictures of the family, save one that was damaged by water. The faces had run and were unrecognizable. A man, a woman, a child.

"There is nobody here," said Henry.

"We should look downstairs," I said.

But neither of us had the nerve. The thing outside seemed foiled by the house, and we did not wish to catch sight of it through a window. The bedroom doors had locks, so we resolved to take to bed and wait out the night. Sunrise would cast a sweeter light on this nightmare and make short work of the fog. I took the master bedroom, and Henry made do with the child's bed.

I confess I cannot imagine how I managed sleep, for I was listening for any sound: the creak of a step, the scrape of a claw, a distant cackle. Yet somehow, consciousness slipped away, and I dreamed of Lizabeth.

It was with Lizabeth haunting my thoughts that I surfaced from slumber. I was still half in and half out of wakefulness, and my mind had not yet caught up with where I was.

There was a body next to me in bed. I felt a presence there, and in my sleep-addled state I took it to be her. How she had come to be there was no concern of mine; perhaps I fancied that I was at home, safe in my room, and that she had at last consented to sleep beside me. I was glad only of her sweet breath and the scent of her. I rolled onto my side and laid my hand lightly upon her cheek, my eyes still closed, drifting back toward slumber.

Reader, what was in the bed next to me that night I dare not fully consider. All I can say is that what my fingers touched then was not the face of my dear beloved. What lay beneath my hand had no skin; I felt wet flesh, teeth, and the moist orb of an eye.

I fear I lost my senses for a time, then. I have little recollection of what came after. There is only a dim nightmare of a ragged shape rising stiffly from the bed as I scrambled away, of long arms reaching out to me as it drifted closer to where I cowered, of a woman's voice heavy with melancholy and bitterness as she breathed a single word.

"Husband."

Then the door burst open and I screamed. A wild-eyed man was grasping me, shaking me. It was only when Henry struck me across the cheek that sanity regained its foothold, and I saw that the wild man was my friend, who looked much affrighted. The apparition—if indeed it had been so and not a trick of my mind—was gone.

"What happened here?" Henry demanded. I babbled my story to him, and he grew grave.

"You have seen something, too!" I realized.

He nodded. "I heard a steady creaking, and fearing that the horror outside might have got in, I went to investigate. But what I saw instead ran my blood cold. There was a man, hung by his neck from the ceiling in the corridor outside my room. As I stood there in shock, he raised his head and glared at me, and then appeared to recede down the corridor, into the shadows."

He clutched my arm. "I know not whether I can trust my own eyes on this, but it seemed to me that *he had your face.*"

A terrible chill gripped me. "This house is a place of madness," I said. "We cannot stay here!"

"But the fog still lingers," Henry said. "We cannot go outside while our pursuer still lurks."

It was then that I became aware of a sound, faint at first but growing louder as my ears fixed upon it. It was the crying of a child.

"Do you hear?" I demanded of Henry.

"I hear it," he said. "Some new evil, no doubt. We should remain here and weather the night in each other's company."

How I wish I had listened to him then. But I could not bear the thought of a child lost in this terrible house. "What if they are trapped here as we are?"

"Then that is their ill fortune," Henry replied. "You must not go wandering. We should wait for the dawn."

But the crying of the child was too much. "I will go," I said. "You can stay, if you must."

"And desert my friend?" he cried. "I think not." But I believe his new gallantry came from the fear of being alone.

We ventured out onto the landing, where Henry had witnessed the terrible sight of the hanged man. Henry had his pistol at the ready now. We heard a soft chuckling from outside and recognized the voice of our unseen pursuer, still prowling the perimeter of the house. I prayed for a swift dawn, then wondered if even the light of the sun would save us.

Henry pointed upward, and I followed his gaze to a hatch in the ceiling. It was from there that the sounds came. We heard muffled movement. There was a child in the attic!

Henry was the taller, so it was he that reached for the key that poked from the lock. For a moment, he hesitated, but he saw the determination in my eyes and steeled himself. I would not leave a child in this hellish place.

He twisted the key, and as he did so, the crying stopped. We heard a scampering toward the far end of the attic, then silence. The hatch fell open with a bang, startling us both. Slowly Henry took the ladder from its hook on the wall and put it into place. We exchanged glances.

I went up first. It was, after all, my decision to find the boy (for a boy it was, I guessed, by the sound of his weeping). Though the moon lit my way, the mouth of the attic was dark, and with each rung of the ladder, I felt my nerves tighten.

I called to the boy as I neared the hatchway. I did not want to go up there. I assured him that we meant no harm, and that he need not be afraid, but I received no answer.

I had no choice, then. Into the pitch-black attic I went.

At first I could see nothing. I waited to be struck by something awful or menaced by some horror alike to the one that had lain in bed beside me. But there was nothing. The boy was hidden and silent.

Eventually my eyes adjusted enough so that I could faintly make out the shape of the attic and its contents. Boxes were piled here and there, and strange mannequins loomed among other debris. Bits of rope, forgotten paintings, and shreds of mouse-eaten sacking occupied the corners.

I saw no sign of the boy, but there were a hundred places to hide. I called again, to no avail. Then my eye fell upon a candelabra resting on a crate. I went gingerly over to it, found a box of matches nearby, and struck one.

The darkness cringed from the flame and shrank back further when I lit the three half-melted candles. Henry, encouraged by the light, peeped up from below, his pistol cocked. But the edges of the room remained dark, and there was still no sign of the boy.

It was then that I noticed the battered journal, which had slipped off the side of the crate. I picked it up and found writing in a young hand. Perhaps this had been where the children of the house had taken themselves to read and write in solitude by candle glow. I searched for the name of the owner and found it on the first page.

HENRY'S JOURNAL.

"What are you doing? Where is the boy?" Henry asked, eager to be gone from there. But my fingers, as if of their own accord, were flipping through the entries in the journal, until I came to the final one. Somehow I sensed there were answers there. Henry clambered up to join me, and together we read.

I am weak now. It seems so long since I have eaten, and my thirst is great. It may be that I cannot hold my quill much longer. Therefore I leave these words to those who may find me here.

There has been no sound from Mother or Father for two days now. Not since Mother locked me up here. She had words to say to Father, she told me, and I was not to hear them. But I heard anyway. I heard her accusing Father of consorting with another woman, with many women. I heard her say that she had borne it so long but would bear it no more. I heard them fight, just below the hatch, and I heard Father strike Mother so hard that she fell.

She did not get up again. I knew that by his tears. He did not mean to kill her. He said so, many times. Perhaps he did not know I was in the attic, above him, listening.

A short while later, I heard his footsteps on the upstairs landing. Then there was a heavy thump, as if a great weight had suddenly fallen. After that, there was only the gentle, swaying creak that I can still hear now.

There is a dog in the house. At least, it sounds like a dog. I can hear it chewing something on the landing. I am terribly afraid. I am afraid that it is eating my mother where she fell.

This will be my last entry. I feel the end is coming soon. May God take me.

"This must be the journal of the boy we heard," I said quietly. "His name was Henry, too."

Henry took it from me and pointed to the top of the page. "It is dated twelve years from now."

I looked closely. He was right. The date was twelve years hence. What did it mean?

I had no time to ponder it, for at that moment a cold wind blew, and the candles guttered and died. We were plunged into utter and complete dark. In the silence that followed, there was only the sound of our breathing. Myself, Henry, . . . and a third pair of lungs.

"What are you doing with my journal?" someone hissed, right by my ear.

Henry shrieked and flung the journal away from him. He staggered across the attic, crying, "Get off me! Get away!" I called out to warn him of the open hatch, but he was insensible with fear. A moment later he was gone, plunging from the attic to land below with a thump and a crack.

"Henry!" I cried, and fled to the edge of the hatch. The ladder had been knocked aside during his fall, and now he lay sprawled, his neck askew. I slipped through the hatch and dropped to his side, tears welling in my eyes, but naught I could do would change the fact that he was dead.

I heard then the malevolent chuckle of a mischievous boy, and as I looked up, I fancied I saw the urchin, his eyes shining in the blackness and his teeth bared. Then the hatch slammed shut.

It was too much for me. Whatever the beast outside, I preferred to meet it than stay another moment in that damned place. So I ran, down the stairs, along the corridor, to the front door.

But the door, when I reached it, would not open. I tugged and pulled and pushed, and finally, defeated, I slumped against it, my forehead pressed to the wood.

The hallway was abominably cold. I knew, by some instinct, what was behind me. But I dared not turn around.

"Husband," she said. *"You have come back."*

"I am nobody's husband," I begged. "I am eighteen years of age, only a boy still. But there is one to whom my heart is pledged, and it is not you."

I drew out then my locket, in which was the likeness of Lizabeth, and I gazed upon it. If I should choose one last thing to see, it would be her. What a fool I was to risk her love by my wanderings, by dalliances with other women who were but a pale shadow of her.

I felt the apparition's breath on my neck, felt her clawed fingers in my hair. But I kept my eyes on the locket, and on Lizabeth, and I asked God to forgive me for squandering such a gift as she was. If I could have one more sight of her, I promised, then she would ever after be enough for me. I pledged myself to her then and there, if I would be delivered from this place.

The apparition's face was next to mine now, the vile wetness of her cheek against me; and still I would not turn, still I would not face her.

"Do not forget me, husband," she said. *"You have been warned."*

And with that, my consciousness deserted me and I fell into a swoon.

I know not where that house came from, nor where it went. I know only that I never saw my dear friend again. I awoke in the woods, on a clear and bright morning, and after a little searching I found the road home and took it. Lizabeth saw to it that I was bathed and put to bed and rested well. I was trying to speak, but she would hear none of it until I was better.

When she deemed me sufficiently recovered, I spoke to her the words I had wanted to say, I think, for much longer than I realized. I had no ring nor any gift to give her, for I could not wait long enough to obtain them; but she did not care for material things. She agreed anyway.

In the days between that and this, I have never told her the story that I have just told to you, dear Reader, and she has never asked. Perhaps she already knows it. I catch her eye sometimes, and in it I see hints of matters that I might never understand: women's ways, dark and strange. It is best that I leave such things undisturbed.

For myself, I do all I can to be a good husband to my beloved. Above all else, I must ensure that what I was warned of on that night shall never come to pass. Not for me, not for Lizabeth, and not for my son, Henry.

Kissing Dead Boys

Annette Curtis Klause

The dead are not very smart. The bouncer, a hulking big vamp, didn't recognize me, although I'd been coming to the bar for weeks. I guessed he'd been dead a long time. The body may be active, but the brain cells keep on decomposing. He just grunted and handed my fake ID back to me, so I blew him a kiss, which he ignored, and swept through the burgundy velvet curtains into the main saloon of Nosferatu.

The walls were black, of course, as were the overstuffed vinyl sofas in half-moon booths lining the walls, ripped from some long-defunct cocktail lounge. Here and there were accents in red—napkins, the stems of cocktail glasses, and intentional graffiti on the wall that dripped out words like *Surrender* and *Despair*. The drone of techno dirge thrummed in the air.

I yanked at the seam of my fishnet stocking and checked out the scene. The bar held fetishists in piercings, tats, and leather; some frilly Victorian types; and fringers in black jeans and whatever, who hadn't quite made up their minds to go goth yet. In the corner was a girl who looked like a reject from a Renaissance fair—except for the white makeup.

Most of the revelers here were human—but not all.

Mundane people think that the goth movement is just a bunch of twisted attention grabbers with black lipstick and an Anne Rice obsession. What they don't know is that some of them really are vampires. What better way to hide—out in the open like that. The majority of the humans here were innocent of the knowledge of whom they drank and danced with; a good few were thrill seekers who had discovered the secret but didn't back off.

Some of the latter went that one step further. They disappeared into dark corners and back rooms and surrendered their veins in return for the creeping sweetness brought on by the vampire's bite, a sweetness that exploded in a gurgling foamy release and left them staggering and wet. It lent a whole new meaning to the retro term *necking*.

A girl with short strawlike hair from a bad blond dye job tottered past me slopping a beer, already tipsy. She wore a telltale scarf to hide the bite marks. It was red to match her skimpy slip dress. The vamps called girls like her blood bags. I'd overheard one say that. He'd probably called me one, too. I wanted to snap his neck.

Blondie arranged herself on a velvet armchair that wouldn't pass inspection in daylight. She patted her hair, loosened her scarf, and tried to look tempting. Yeah, yeah—the Queen of the Damned. *You're fooling yourself*, I thought. Her kind confused the ecstasy of anesthesia with power over death. They reveled in being wanted, of having something the vamps craved, and thought they had the upper hand. They should just enjoy the high. They'd be safer that way.

I leaned against a column papered with concert flyers and misspelled personals, lit a cigarette with my favorite Zippo lighter, and looked for the undead.

How do you tell the real vamps from the wannabes? It has nothing to do with who wears a crucifix and who doesn't. Crucifixes don't burn the undead—perhaps they never did. The vamps wear them with ironic insolence. What tips you off is the dark blank eyes, like those of sharks—that and the dry tongue. Vampires don't have much in the way of fluids in them when they haven't had a meal for a while. If I actually kissed a vampire with a wet tongue, I'd be worried about what he had in his mouth. That didn't bear thinking about closely.

It was early yet—only four of them here. I exhaled a long stream of smoke. One male was an albino who looked too old to be hanging out in this bar. He reminded me of a white rat in a suit. The others were probably too old, too, but at least they didn't look it—two females who weren't disgusting or anything, but I don't go that way, and a male who was just too dorky. I'm sorry, but platform shoes? Someone needed to tell him that disco was deader than he was. If I'm going to kiss a dead boy, he'd better be a babe, or else I can't overcome the gross factor. I'd wait. There would be more soon.

It had taken me a while to discover this bar—it wasn't the sort of place most people would find readily or come to willingly—but one night I followed my sister into a dank alley and down a short flight of steps that stank of urine, to a rotting side door under a carved red swinging sign. Yes, I had to follow my little sister to find this place. It still irked me that she had known about the secret nightlife of the city and I hadn't. That she was cooler than me.

My younger sister and I always had a love-hate relationship, but it was mostly love until she turned thirteen and evil. Then nothing anyone said was right. She snarled at all of us. It was like her existence was one huge sunburn. Even her best friend stopped calling. "What crawled up your ass and died?" I asked her one day. I stopped asking any such thing after she chased me around the house with a steak knife and I had to climb out the bathroom window to escape. I hid in the garden shed where we'd once played cavemen and, okay, I cried. I didn't recognize this creature she'd become.

Send her to a shrink, I told my parents. But that was too embarrassing for them to consider. That was admitting defeat. That was saying they couldn't control their young. Thanks. They didn't have to share a bedroom with her.

One night I woke up to find my sister climbing out our bedroom window. I pretended to be asleep still, but after she left, I followed her. She met a boy by the garage and they groped in the moonlight. I was going to back off, not wanting to witness her latest episode of juvenile delinquency, but something he said stopped me. "Your blood is sweet, so sweet," he murmured. He buried his head in her neck, and she clutched his shoulders with white-knuckled hands. I backed away slowly and ducked into the shadow of Dad's car, which was parked in the driveway. She was reflected in the side mirror, he was not.

After that, I sometimes noticed the holes in her neck before she wrapped it with a black chiffon scarf in her daily ritual, and I glimpsed suspicious scars on her arms whenever her long black sleeves rode up.

Vampires were real. I saw that then. But did he come to her because she was already evil, or had he sensed the rebellion and anger in her and sought her out and made her evil? Had the way she'd been acting lately something to do with him?

I remembered the baggy-kneed kid she had once been with a bowl haircut and floppy bangs, wearing a pirate-like patch to correct a lazy eye. We had flown to the stars behind an upturned coffee table and galloped down the street on imaginary horses. Was it safe for her to meet this creature? Could she handle herself? Should I tell my parents? Some misguided loyalty to a sibling stopped me, despite the way she scorned me now. Or perhaps it was fear of retribution. I thought of that knife and my narrow escape out the bathroom window. Perhaps *he* should be worried about *her*. Part of me was repelled by what she was doing with the vamp and part of me was intrigued. I was also angry. She was younger! How come she attracted a vampire and not me? Even my friends commented on how cute she was, and here she was upstaging me again. It was all very sexy and secret, and it wasn't happening to me. Where did she find a vampire? Where could I get one?

I began to spy on her. I followed her here.

The bar had filled up. People were dancing now— grinding against each other to the mechanical insistence of the music. The predator noses of the vamps were no doubt inhaling the salty seduction of sweat and sexual juices, intimate nectars that come so close to blood. The new vamps I spotted arriving would probably have been drooling if they'd had enough water in them. As I stubbed my cigarette out on the stained floor, I saw a redheaded bitch drag a willing boy by his hair into the shadows. He was oblivious to the wicked leer on her face.

The vamps that didn't feel like dinner yet hung close together like the hot kids in high school. They blew out the candles on the tables they occupied—they didn't like open flames—and they sat in front of brightly colored cocktails that they never touched, ignoring the stares of those who wanted to entice immortality. People like me. My pick-up moves might work on one alone, but I didn't want an audience that might laugh and blow my chance, an audience that would remember me later. I had to catch one cruising. I watched the solo vamps who went on fishing trips among the potential blood donors. None of them tickled my fancy.

Then someone new pushed through the velvet curtains from the entrance hall. The slim young man with a long black braid would have caught my eye even if I hadn't been trolling for vamps. He wore his black frock coat as if he really had been an eighteenth-century highwayman. His dark, cold eyes suggested there was truth to that. His face was pale, but not with makeup. He examined the crowd with an arrogant gaze. When he walked across the dance floor, the dancers made room for him automatically, as if he had control of the blood within their veins and was parting the Red Sea. He found an empty seat away from the other vamps and flung his booted legs up on the table with a clanking thud I heard over the music. After he shot a scornful look at the cluster of his undead fellows, he examined his nails and pretended not to stare at the live girls. He was a loner. I would bet he wasn't used to bar pickups but was desperate enough for blood to come here tonight. I licked my lips. This was the one.

I slipped the pin from the lapel of my black silk shirt and pricked the side of my neck, just under my ear. I yanked the pin as I pulled it out, to make sure there was blood—it only took a little to catch their attention. I tucked the pin back where it belonged and sauntered toward the bar—past the highwayman. *Get a whiff of me, honey,* I thought. *Don't I smell gooooooooooood?* I didn't look, but I could almost feel his eyes on me. I smiled to myself.

The bartender was new—human, Lord save him. The trouble with vampires hiring human bartenders is that sooner rather than later, the drink maker looks better than the drinks. Nosferatu went through more bartenders than cocktail napkins.

"I'll have two Suicides," I told him.

He raised his eyebrows. "You *do* know that's 151-proof rum and a few drops of lemon juice?"

"Whatever."

He shrugged. It was on the doorman, not him, if I was underage. "Two?"

"One for my friend over there." I nodded toward the vamp hottie who was dutifully looking back as if I really were with him. I'd caught his attention all right.

"Oh, he's not going to drink that," the bartender said with a knowing grin. Maybe he'd last longer around here than the others.

"Then more for me," I said, glaring. The bartender was cute, with his little halfhearted goatee. In earlier days, I might have tried to hook up with *him*. He put the drinks on the bar, and I rummaged through my army-surplus shoulder bag for my wallet—too much junk, cigarettes, lighter fluid, nail-polish remover, rubbing alcohol—then I handed over more money from my salary as a shelving assistant at the local library than I'd like to. Someone cranked up the music another notch.

I took the drinks and approached my prey. He scowled and glanced around as if looking for an exit. A pushy girl amused some vamps, but he seemed the type who would prefer the upper hand. Okay, I'd give it to him. Right before I reached him, I pretended to trip. The drinks went flying—right down the front of his highwayman's coat.

He jumped to his feet with a curse, sending his chair crashing. I heard laughter from humans at a nearby table.

"Oh, God! Oh, God! I'm so sorry," I gushed. I had to speak loudly to be heard over the music. "I'm such a jerk. I'm so clumsy." I tried to dab at his jacket with a Kleenex and only managed to leave tiny balls of paper down his front. "Oh, shit!"

He smiled. He liked that. I wasn't the forward harlot in control of the situation anymore. I was a loser. He could deal with losers. He brushed at his coat with his fingers, then shrugged and grinned. He leaned close to speak in my ear. "It was an accident," he said magnanimously. He had a deep voice that sounded somewhat hollow. He must have caught another whiff of blood, because his dark eyes narrowed with cunning. "You must let me buy you another drink." He conveniently ignored the fact that I had been carrying two.

"Maybe I've had enough," I answered, and giggled. "Well, perhaps a Coke."

He gestured to a chair and I sat, then he waved the bartender over, even though people don't do that at Nosferatu; they get their own drinks from the bar. The bartender came anyway and took his order—one Coke for me. The vamp didn't even make a pretense of wanting a drink.

Then we didn't talk, but he was fine with that. He just stared at me. They do that—stare. His stare was sultry and worthy of a pinup boy. His gaze made me feel all warm. I relaxed into the pounding music and enjoyed it. He was using his hypnotic powers to make me horny. *Thanks, buddy. I'd go with you anyway, but— yum!* I giggled, and it was only half put on.

I was fidgety with nerves and shoved my hands under my thighs to keep them still. My Coke came and I grabbed it tight and sipped, then I took a deep breath to project my voice. "I haven't seen you here before." I gritted my teeth. That line was only half an inch off from *Do you come here often?*

"No, you haven't," returned Mr. Conversational.

I wanted to get to the point. I wanted to say, *Come outside to the alley with me, dead boy,* but something told me he wouldn't go unless *he* invited *me.* I tilted my head in a way I hoped looked innocently flirtatious, but which really whispered, *Ooooooh, look at the deeeeee-licious neck.* "It's kinda loud in here, isn't it?" I said. "It's hard to have a conversation."

"Would you like to go somewhere quieter?" he asked.

I stifled a grin and nodded. He rose to his feet and offered me his hand. I stood up, too, grabbing my bag. Then he looked around, a little lost. He hadn't been here before.

"This way," I mouthed, and tugged his fingers. I led him to a side door, and he followed silently and quickly. He was embarrassed to be here. He didn't want anyone to see us leave. I liked that. I liked discreet.

He was surprised to find himself in the alley, but I shrugged. "It's a nice night, and it's private out here," I said as I slid my bag from my shoulder and dropped it to the ground.

He smiled and pulled me to him. Our eyes met, and I could tell he knew that I knew and that we had forged a contract. I loved the way he smiled. What a pity he was dead. He covered my mouth with his, and his kiss was pretty good really. His mouth was dry, but it didn't taste bad—minty, in fact. I choked back a laugh. He'd brushed his teeth; how thoughtful. He was a gentleman vampire.

I wriggled invitingly in his arms. *Come on*, I thought, impatient for the main course. He smelled a little musty. It had probably been a while since that coat had seen a dry cleaner, if ever, and sleeping in dirt didn't help, but I'd smelled much worse, and the payoff would be worth it.

He held me close and deepened his kiss. Finally, his lips went to my neck while his hands took liberties intended to distract me. A shiver of fear trembled up my spine as I felt his fangs snicker through my flesh. I always shivered no matter how many times I did this. *Just stay aware*, I told myself as the warmth began to suffuse me—hot, hot, hotter in his cold, cold arms. His hand was under my skirt. A little moan of pleasure escaped my lips. He was good—very good. I gasped a shallow little triple-tiered breath, and I almost lost control. He went further than they usually did. They usually forgot about me as soon as they tasted blood. They had a meal; I had a cheap thrill—that was it. The exchange was usually over by now.

My knees were weak. He'd drunk a lot of my blood, enough that when he ground against me, he felt like a real man. I suddenly knew what he intended. He would take me, and not the way romance novels mean it. He would screw me for real and suck all my blood as he did, and I wanted him to. I had never felt so hot for someone, vamp or human. He would kill me and I'd enjoy it. Like my sister had.

My little sister.

Then I felt bile rise in the back of my throat and sting me to my senses. "Hey," I mumbled. "You've had enough. This isn't how it works." I tried to push him away, but his icy arms tightened around me like iron bands. He wasn't letting go. My neck muffled his laughter as he tore at my skirt. I had slipped. I had let it go too far. I tried to beat on his face with my left hand, but he grabbed my arms and pinned them to my sides. If I didn't get away, I would be dead for sure. I struggled furiously, but I was trapped and weak. I could feel him sucking the life out of me, and the pleasure I'd felt not so long ago was just a fading itch.

I went limp. The creature moaned with pleasure and sucked at me like a leech. He had won. He knew. His grip loosened slightly.

I managed to wiggle my fingers into my skirt pocket. There was a faint chance. I maneuvered out my lighter and silently begged my fingers not to fumble and drop it. My hand was numb from his grip. At first, my thumb wouldn't cooperate and my heart nearly burst with panic. Then I heard the familiar *ching* as I flipped the lid open and then my thumb found the wheel. He hissed and let me go abruptly, drawing his singed hand to his mouth. I jumped back, holding the lighter in front of me, its acrid flickering blue flame my only hope. Good thing about Zippos: once they're lit, they're lit; you don't have to hold anything down. Bad thing about Zippos— they burn your fingers if you hold them too long.

I flung the lighter at him—flung it onto the rotten dry coat I had deliberately doused with alcohol. A filmy sheet of flame ran up the jacket, and the vamp snarled in surprise. It wasn't enough. The flames weren't strong enough. In a moment, he'd shrug the coat off and be on me again. His eyes sparkled with rage. His bared fangs dripped with my blood. I had to do something fast.

I dived for my bag. The first thing I grabbed was a plastic bottle—nail-polish remover. I aimed and squeezed, and it shot liquid better than a water pistol. The flames roared. *Ahhh!* A shoulder bag full of accelerants is a girl's best friend. He had no time to scream.

I was panting and my heart was thumping, but my whole core thrummed with triumph. They went up quickly, these vamps. They were all dried-up and dead— dry as tinder. He'd soon be a pile of ashes, and no one would know he'd been there at all.

Holy water didn't work—I'd sprinkled some surreptitiously one busy night at the bar and not one vampire sizzled. Sunlight you had to wait for and be in the right place, and I couldn't trust myself to be strong enough with a stake. How do you practice? How do you know you can ram it through a chest, even an old vampire chest?

It came down to fire. I could do that.

I used to be curious about the vamps. I thought the blood bags were skanky and funny, but there was something intriguing about that quick, anonymous, not quite sex, something enticing about walking that thin line between pleasure and danger. But I didn't dare do it. I didn't dare try it. And why should I? It was asking for trouble. But when I wasn't feeling superior, I was jealous that my sister walked fearlessly where I could not, angry that she seemed so assured, so in control.

Everything changed the night I found her dead behind a Dumpster.

That's when I realized she hadn't been in control at all. She'd been playing a stupid game and I was too much of an asshole to stop her when I'd had a chance. I didn't tell on her. I unthinkingly let her run headfirst into danger. It was too late now, but I had to do something. I had to find the courage after all.

I picked up my lighter and shook off the ash with trembling fingers. Nowadays, I think of myself as pest control.

It's a challenge, really, to see how many I can get before they get me. I like to think that they will never catch on. It's fun in a way. I suppose I could be out doing drugs or cutting myself or something, but this seems more productive in the long run.

This is my job—kiss the dead boys, then put them away. This is my tribute to my sister.

This is for Julie.

The Heart of Another

Marcus Sedgwick

When I woke. The first thing. Was. The Light.

It was there even before. Even before I had my eyes open. Then. I made the mistake. Of opening my eyes.

Light filled my head and I was blinded.

I didn't know where I was. Of course. I knew nothing. It was all so hard. Even to think. Never mind to remember.

I shut my eyes. Quickly.

Slowly.

Ever so slowly, things began to change. I began to think, and I began to remember.

I realized where I was. The hospital. I could smell it now, and though my eyes were shut, I could see the hospital. My white room. All around me would be wards and nurses. Doctors.

The next thing was the pain.

Everything was a blur. My head was throbbing. My arms and legs were jelly, but somewhere there was a vast pain.

Gingerly, I moved one of my jelly arms underneath the bedclothes. I lifted a hand up across my chest, catching one breast, pulling on something.

A pain speared through my chest and the white light went black.

I don't know how long it was before I woke again.

It was dark now, and for a moment I thought I'd gone blind somehow. That was the first time I began to panic. Not because I thought I'd gone blind, but because I knew I was thinking irrationally. But maybe it was a good sign. Maybe it was the first time I'd been well enough to think, even if those thoughts were irrational.

It might have been the evening of the same day I first woke. It might have been a week later. I had no way of telling.

I could still feel the pain between my breasts, and this time, I moved carefully, lifting my jelly hand high, and then inching it back toward my chest.

Yes, there it was. A thick dressing running down my breastbone. I rested a finger on it as lightly as I could. The pain howled into me again and I lay back on the pillow, cowering, waiting for the sharpness to return to a dull ache.

A single word floated into my head, and I knew it was a word that had been spoken over my unconscious body, many times, like a prayer. An invocation.

The word was a strange one. *Cyclosporine.*

I tried it on my tongue, whispering into the dark.

"Cyclo. Sporine."

I couldn't remember what it meant, but I knew it was of enormous importance to me. Now.

I lay in the dark. Waiting for someone to come.

No one came.

Before I knew I was asleep, I found myself waking again.

The pain was less. And now real thoughts ran through me. Real thoughts. The ones that make us human. Desires and fears.

My first fear was for my work. Ever since they found when I was a child that I had a bad heart, I suppose I'd been waiting for the operation to happen. And it had to happen seventeen years later, just as I was trying to get my thesis together. The last year had been a mess, as my heart that had never been made properly started to give out.

There'd been a few scares. I nearly didn't make it a couple of times. But I kept working when I could. It was only thanks to John, my tutor, that I'd gotten anywhere at all. But my parents had been pressing for the operation— I knew that. I knew I couldn't fight it off forever, though

I didn't want to admit it. "The Speculations of Edgar Allan Poe" would have to wait.

I told my parents I didn't want to interrupt my thesis, but the real reason was simpler than that. I was scared. Finally I couldn't hold out anymore, but things weren't that simple. I'd only been thinking about me, what I wanted and what I didn't want. But I'd forgotten that for the operation to happen at all, we needed something else.

A compatible thing.

Of the right tissue type.

And it seemed that in the whole Bay Area, no one was dying with the kind of heart I needed. So I lay in the hospital, getting closer and closer to death.

Until finally someone died, and saved me.

At some point they'd removed the dressing from my chest, and now I could run my fingers down the scar. Miserably I wondered if it would ever heal well enough so it didn't show. It would be something to explain to my boyfriend, if I ever had one. And as I pondered a sex life I might never have, a different kind of desire crept into me.

Suddenly, from nowhere, came an overwhelming need for a long, cool glass of beer.

Which was very strange because I have always hated beer.

* * *

Those first days seem so far away now. It was a strange time. A long blur of light and dark, of pain and numbness. Things are much clearer now. I can think again. In fact, I was thinking clearly well before I was allowed out. That was the worst time. So frustrating, when all I wanted to do was get back to my work.

My parents came to see me during that time. I'd asked them to bring my books. At the very least, I begged for Poe's *Tales of Mystery and Imagination*. Yes, I'd read them all a dozen times, but I still had to focus myself on them. On him. They brought me no books. They brought me a magazine.

Mother looked worried. Dad looked at Mother, almost as if I weren't there.

"Are you taking your pills?" Mother said.

"What do you think?" I snapped, then regretted it. She began to wring her hands. I knew she felt my condition was her fault. And maybe it was.

"They bring it in three times a day," I said, trying to be nicer. "Twenty-five milligrams of cyclosporine. There's no way I'll be allowed to forget."

"You need it, darling."

I smiled at them and told them I was fine.

They left. I threw the magazine across the room, then collapsed on my pillows, wincing.

A couple of days later I had another visitor. John Reynolds, my tutor. He was even taller than I remembered him, but otherwise he was your average professor of English. Middle-aged. Messy hair, poor dress sense. Good-looking, though, I admit.

"You look well," he said, smiling down at me. I could tell he was lying, but it was good of him to say it.

I waved a hand limply.

"Yeah, you know. . . ."

He said nothing. Just stared at me.

"So where were you, John? I've been here for days, and—"

He held up his hand.

"I'm sorry," he said. "I'm sorry. I was at the Funkdorf Convention in Geneva. I told you all April was pretty much wiped out. Got back two days ago. There was a lot to do. . . ."

I said nothing, still angry at him for abandoning me.

"I have something for you," he said, and pulled a book from his bag.

"How did you know?"

I forgot to be angry anymore; it was the *Tales of Mystery and Imagination.*

"Let's just say I guessed. Don't think I want you working hard. You need to take it easy. But you're the best student I've ever had, and that thesis won't wait forever. A little light reading until you're ready to get back to Edgar properly."

I smiled and put the book down on the bed beside me. It had become too heavy to hold.

"Do you know where you're going to take it yet?"

I laughed.

"I thought you didn't want me working hard."

He shrugged. "Just a question."

"Well, I think I'm going to try to pull one of the tales apart. Break it down and build it up again. I'm going to analyze sentence structure, paragraph length, and vocab. But more important than that, I'm going to propose that you can find the essence of Poe in any of his stories. His style, his ideas, his structures. That everything that is him is to be found in all his work. Like a fingerprint."

"Sounds good," John said. "Sounds very good. But which tale are you going to use?"

"'The Tell-Tale Heart,'" I said, and even as I said it, I knew it had to be that one. That was a strange thing, because up to that point I had had no idea.

John shrugged.

"Okay," he said. He turned to the window—a little awkwardly, I thought.

"Soon be summer," he said.

"Perfect for a fishing trip across the bay," I said.

He turned from the window.

"What?"

"Nothing," I said.

"I didn't know you liked fishing."

"I don't," I said. "I just thought . . ."

I trailed off. John said nothing.

He made to leave.

"You're taking your cyclosporine?"

I laughed.

"Yes," I said.

"You know you need it, so your body . . . accepts your new heart."

"Yes," I said, but still smiling patiently. "I get that lecture three times a day from the nurses."

He went.

I looked down at the book he'd brought me. I put a hand on it, but I was too tired to pick it up.

I closed my eyes, and then it hit me.

Yes. I had to take my cyclosporine because the heart in my chest wasn't mine, and my body might reject it otherwise.

It might reject it because it came from someone else.

I had someone else's heart inside me, and the heart of another is a dark forest.

"The Tell-Tale Heart." Once I'd said it to John, it had to be that story. It had everything I needed for my thesis, and I knew it would yield to the rigorous analysis I had planned for it. But why that story? There were others just as useful for my purposes.

The story features a wild narrator, obsessive, and yet his narration displays an apparent logic. The narrator kills the old man in whose house he lodges and carries off the deed with chilling efficiency. He seems to have gotten away with the crime, and even when the police come to search the house, having heard reports of a shriek, he convinces them that all is well. But the narrator is convinced that he can still hear the old man's heart beating. The beating gets louder and louder, and the killer can't understand why the police can't hear it. Finally his mind snaps and he confesses—pointing toward the floorboards where the old man's body lies.

What he never understands is why the police seem to be ignoring the loud and frantic beating of the heart.

The narrator is, of course, mad.

And the thing about madmen is that they don't know they're mad.

The dreams started when I got home. My initial delight at being freed from the hospital died that very first night. It had been awful, stuck in that white, white room, for day after day after day. I read the *Tales of Mystery and Imagination* from cover to cover so many times I lost count. When I got a little stronger, I began to make notes for my thesis, but nothing could prevent the awful spaces of boredom that filled my days.

My parents drove me home and walked slowly beside me as I made my way up the stairs. Three flights and I was exhausted, but I put on a brave face so they wouldn't worry, and after a while, I managed to get them to leave.

As soon as they'd gone, I collapsed on the sofa and slept all afternoon. When I woke, it was dusk. I got up for a bit and wandered around my apartment as if it belonged to someone else. It had been so long; everything was unfamiliar and so different from the whiteness of the room. At first it was hard to take it all in. The colors, the browns—chairs, my desk, the floorboards. The spines of books on the shelves. The shiny things in the kitchen, the soft things in the bedroom.

After an hour of this aimlessness, I felt overwhelmed by tiredness again and went to bed. I undressed and looked at myself naked in the bedroom mirror. The scar was much better, but I knew then that it would always be there. I pulled on a nightshirt and went to bed. And that's when the dreams started.

The first thing is the pain. Pain searing across my chest. Then there is the light, not bright and all-encompassing, but a single beam blazing in a darkened space. Then there's the crack as my breastbone is split in two. By now I should have passed out from the pain, but I don't. I see a knife slide into me, slitting the pericardium. My heart is exposed. Someone reaches their hands toward it.

That's when I wake, screaming.

It's what I'd been thinking deep down but had refused to acknowledge. My heart is not my own. Yes, it's true that they left in a small piece of my own weak organ, but the thing that does the work now, that pumps my blood, is someone else's. It's something I haven't wanted to think about, but I can't push it away anymore.

I wonder whose it was.

Man or woman? How old were they? And, the one question that for some reason bothers me the most— how did they die?

And supposing, just supposing, this dead person isn't happy that I've got their heart. Suppose they want it back?

I got a little stronger each day, but having been confined to that white room for so long, I now found myself confined to my own apartment. I had to arrange to have groceries delivered, because I didn't even have the strength to get to the corner shop and back. So I stayed at my desk, reading "The Tell-Tale Heart" again and again.

And just as I had told John, I pulled it apart. I think, in fact, I dissected it, like a surgeon with a scalpel. I came to know every word. I produced ratios of word length to sentence length, sentence length to paragraph length. I distilled Edgar Allan Poe to a sequence of numbers. But my frustration grew, because despite all my analysis, I felt no closer to being able to write a single word of my thesis.

John would stop by from time to time, bring me books I needed from the library, return those I had finished with.

One day, he looked at me strangely.

"What's wrong?" he said, so simply that I couldn't keep it in any longer. I told him about the dreams. It all flooded out and I felt like a fool, but he listened seriously.

"It's not that hard to understand," he said when I had finished. "You had a major surgical operation—just about as big as they come in fact. What you're having is an anxiety dream about the operation."

Even as he said it, I knew that wasn't quite right, but I felt better for having unburdened myself, and I decided to let it drop.

"What I need," I said, "is a drink. Want a beer?"

He stood up, smiling.

"Thanks," he said. "But I've got too much work to mark from students less able than you."

I blushed and showed him out.

When he'd gone, I thought about what he'd said.

There was something wrong with it; I just couldn't place it.

Not yet.

But that night, when I had the dream yet again and woke, I woke without screaming, because I had realized that the dream wasn't about me at all. It was about him—the man who'd died and whose heart I was now in possession of.

Even as I woke, I'd woken somehow knowing that it was a man's heart.

* * *

Days went by, and I got stronger. I still had the dreams, but they no longer scared me. Every night, without fail, I found myself reliving the same sequence. At first I had found it terrifying, then only disturbing, then just unpleasant. The fact was the operation I experienced nightly was not my own, but the man's; his heart was being removed to give to me. The two processes were almost the mirror of each other; it was just that mine was a little less brutal than his. A little.

And as the nights passed, my horror became transformed into something else: sympathy.

One day, as I'd spent all morning at my desk and failed to do anything productive at all, something suddenly happened to me. I stared at the work in front of me, and it was dull and boring. I pushed it away, slid my chair from the desk, and walked to the window. I pulled the curtains wide, and light flooded into the room. It was a burning summer's day, and I threw the windows open so sharply they slammed against the walls outside.

There was the whole city in front of me, and beyond, I could see the sun glinting on the sea. I imagined what it would be like to take a boat out across the bay and feel the water and the sun and the wind. What it would be like to pull a bright wet fish into the bottom of the boat and see it flap.

I left the apartment for the first time.

That day was incredible to me.

All my life, I'd labored with a failing heart. I'd never walked farther than a mile before, and yet, that day, I walked clear across the city and down to the bay. I swam in a small cove I discovered, and I never even stopped to think that I'd never learned to swim.

It got dark before I returned, and still I could have kept on walking. I felt stronger than I'd ever felt, and for the first time I appreciated what an amazing gift I'd been given. I had been given a life that had been closed to me before.

I was a new person. Thanks to a dead man.

My euphoria was short-lived, however, because that night was when the darkness rolled in. I had a different dream, and it was terrible. This wasn't a dream about the autopsy anymore; this was a dream about how he died. He wasn't an old man. He was a young man. I felt it all as if I were there, as if I were him. He was a young man, and he didn't die easily or from an accident.

He was killed.

He was murdered.

I woke, and I cried until dawn.

Days passed. I looked at my work less and less, and spent more and more time outside. Walking, running. I got myself a gym membership, and I became stronger. As I ran, I would think about him. My life giver. The man whose heart I was using to full capacity. I felt such sorrow for him, yet how could I regret what had happened? For without it, I would be dead.

One day, out running, I passed the city library, and something clicked in my head. Something inside the building screamed at me, and I felt a tug that I hadn't felt in weeks—the desire to learn, the desire to study, the desire to know.

Inside, I knew right away where the pull was coming from. I sailed up to the third floor—the floor where few people go—to the periodical collections.

Four months ago, more or less. April 15.

I began to read, slowly at first, but then more and more frantically. I found something in the *Gazette*. Then another story in the *Bay Times*. Then with a shock I found another one a few days before. I went further back and found one weeks before that.

My heart grew cold.

I grabbed all the papers I wanted to look at again and walked downstairs and straight out of the library, ignoring the old lady at the desk shouting at me.

I went home and spread everything out on the floor. I discarded all the pages of the papers I didn't need, and yet there were still enough to fill the living-room floor. A carpet of death.

The intercom buzzed, and I nearly hit the ceiling.

"Yes?" I said impatiently.

"It's John."

"Thank God," I said. "If it had been Mother . . ."

I buzzed the door.

A minute later he was in my apartment.

"What are you doing?" he asked, seeing the paper on the floor.

I shrugged.

"Are you all right?" he asked.

"Yes, fine. Why?"

He hesitated.

"I haven't see you at school, and . . ."

"You know I've been stuck here," I began, but even as I said it, I knew it was a stupid thing to say.

"You've been seen everywhere around the city. Running. Everywhere, but at college."

"You're hurt?" I said. He had such a stupid look on his face, as if he cared about me.

"We haven't seen a word of your thesis. Time is running out."

"I'm working on it." I said defensively.

"Is this part of it?" John said, waving a hand at the cuttings from the papers.

"No, but . . ."

"I stuck my neck out for you, because I believe you are the best student I've ever had. With all your health problems over the years, it wasn't easy. I just need to see some results. Some work."

I said nothing. What could I say? I was guilty. I'd been well enough to run five miles every morning, but I hadn't opened a book in weeks.

"What is all this, anyway?" John asked.

I saw a chance to excuse myself.

"Don't start," I said. "It's not been easy. The operation has changed me. I dream . . ."

"They haven't stopped?"

"No. They've gotten worse. Listen, John, the thing is. About my heart. I've dreamed about my heart. I know how I got it. It was murder, John. *Murder!* It's been filling my brain—I couldn't concentrate on Poe anymore. I went to the library and found all these."

"What are they?"

I could see him looking at me strangely.

"Murders. Reports of murders in the area. Around the time of my operation. Young people, in every case. There's even a story about the high number of murders that had been happening, more than normal. The police were baffled, it says."

"What of it?"

"One of them is mine. One of them is my heart. I think I know which one. It all makes sense. . . ."

John shifted and moved around the floor, looking at the paper cuttings. He shook his head.

"I think maybe you've been working too hard," he said.

"You've just told me I haven't been working at all!" I shouted suddenly.

"Listen, I just think you've been through a lot. This is all very fascinating stuff, but you shouldn't think about it like this."

"Why not?" I snapped. "Why shouldn't I? Someone died for me! Someone was murdered! Without that fact, I'd be dead. I just want to know who it was."

John raised his hand, trying to calm me down.

"Don't be like this," he said. "Please. You shouldn't upset yourself. Like I said before, a heart transplant is a major operation and some . . . mental trauma afterward is only natural."

"You don't believe me?"

"It's not a question of whether I believe you. I just think you should leave the man who died out of this. It won't do any good. . . ."

"What did you say?"

John said nothing, and I knew he was replaying what he had said.

"How did you know it was a man?" I asked. "I didn't tell you that."

"What—?" he said quickly. "It was . . . just a guess. An assumption."

But I knew he was lying. In that moment, I knew.

I bent over and picked up one of the pages, and I read, all the while keeping an eye on John's face.

"'Police today are investigating the apparently motiveless murder of a young man from the city area. The man's wallet was still on his person, including money, plastic, and even his donor card. The twenty-four-year-old was found in the early hours of yesterday morning, killed by a single shot to the head. He was a dockworker, from the fishing houses, and a fitness fanatic, according to his friends, one of whom said, "I can't believe he won't be there for a beer after work, like usual." Police say they have no leads at present.'"

Then I knew for sure.

I looked at John.

You're my best student—that's what he'd said.

"How many did you have to kill, John? I was at the top of the waiting list for a heart. How many did you have to kill before they found one with the right tissue type?"

"Don't be absurd. . . ."

"Did you ask them if they had a donor card before you killed them?"

"The Tell-Tale Heart." Remember that story—the one with the mad narrator? My heart had told a tale. My heart had found its murderer. He tried to deny it. He grabbed the clipping from my hand as we argued. He looked at the date. He tried to tell me that he was at the convention in Geneva when the dockworker had been murdered. But I didn't believe him. He must have set it all up somehow. Oh, yes, I knew better than to fall for that.

I.

Knew.

He told me I was mad, that I'd lost my mind.

But I know I'm not mad.

Not.

Me.

But there's something I don't know.

I don't really know which of us did it.

I know it was me who caught John by the arm as he tried to leave the apartment. And it was me who held him on the floor while my hands closed around his neck and stayed there until he stopped shuddering.

But I don't know whether it was me or my heart that really killed him.

I guess the police will decide.

John was a tall man. And strong.

A small woman. Like me.

Could never. Have killed someone.

Like him.

Could she?

The Necromancers

Herbie Brennan

"Look," Tar said, thumbing through a spotty copy of the *Lemegeton* they'd found in a junk shop, "there's a picture here."

Wit leaned across. It was a faded print of small artistic merit pasted onto one of the pages and probably every bit as old as the book itself. It showed two bearded men in Elizabethan costume sharing a circle with a funny-looking woman in a nightgown, bed socks, and a bed cap. The scene beyond the circle was one of gloomy trees and tombstones. A hand-lettered caption said, *"Dr. Dee and Edward Kelley Question a Spirit in Highgrove Graveyard."*

"That's what we want to do," Tar said. "Question a spirit."

"Do you think she was really dead?" Wit asked, frowning. "She looks as if they might just have gotten her out of bed."

Tar shook his head soberly. "No, they buried you in clothes like that in those days. *Not dead but only sleeping,*" he quoted. "I saw it on an old tombstone. They dressed you for bed, then buried you."

"I've often wondered why spirits wear clothes at all," Wit said. "You'd think they'd have nothing on. Like babies."

"Yaaaas," said his brother, who wasn't really listening. He turned a page and the Highgrove picture was replaced by a drawing of a magic circle, not pasted in this time, but printed in the book. It looked fearfully complicated, with weird signs and holy names around the rim. One of them was JESVS, which mightn't be a lot of good if your spirit was Jewish. "Do you think this sort of thing could really work?" he asked.

"Only one way to find out," said Wit.

Tar was short for Tarquin. Wit was named for Wittgenstein, the philosopher. Oddly enough, Tar was the more thoughtful twin. "You see," he said as he tied a piece of chalk to one end of the string, "all these preparations—the circle and the fasting and the prayers and stuff—all these may be just a way of influencing your mind—like, making you hallucinate. There's nutmeg in that incense. Nutmeg's a psychedelic."

"Yeah, right," said Wit, and grinned.

With one of them at each end of the string, they drew a nine-foot circle on the cellar floor, then shortened it a handsbreadth and drew a second circle inside the first. The chalk snapped in half just as they were finishing.

"Do you think that's an omen?" Wit asked anxiously.

Tar shook his head. "No." He got busy writing the holy names. "You do the sigils," he said over his shoulder. "You're better at drawing than me."

It was nearly midnight by the time they'd finished, but their circle looked the business. "I wish Cassandra could see this," Wit said. Cassandra was a girl they both fancied. So far she hadn't said which one she fancied back, probably because she couldn't tell the difference between them. It was an old problem for the twins.

"Cassandra wouldn't approve," Tar said. "She was terribly religious before she got her belly button pierced."

Wit was looking at the book. "We have to do a triangle now," he said gloomily. It had been a long day and they were both tired.

"Let's not," Tar said. "Dr. Dee and Edward Kelley didn't have a triangle." He was talking about the pasted picture.

Wit wasn't convinced. "It says here it's *dangerous* if you try to do it without the triangle."

"That's demons," Tar told him. "We're not calling up demons; we're just raising Grandpa. He won't do us any harm."

"Do you think he'll tell us where he hid the money?"

"Of course he will," Tar said with confidence. "He loves us, and he loves Mum and Dad—Mum's his *daughter*, cripes' sake. Besides, money's not much good to him where he is now."

"Where he is now?" asked Wit curiously. "You mean, like, heaven—?"

"I mean like dead," Tar said.

It was three minutes after midnight when they began the ceremony. Tar lit the nutmeg incense, and Wit read the evocation. It was supposed to call some big-deal devil named Lucifuge Rofocal, so he substituted Grandpa's name. Wit read things very well, but nothing happened.

After a moment, Tar said, "Read it again."

Wit read it again and this time did something right because a funny cloud formed inside the circle.

"Is that you, Grandpa?" Tar asked, peering.

There was a curious *straining* in the air and, distantly, the sound of Mozart's *Requiem*, although that might possibly have come from the stereo upstairs. The atmosphere thickened to the point where Wit felt as if he'd started to breathe soup. Then he heard a distinct *pop* and a familiar figure stepped out of the funny cloud.

"Grandpa!" Wit said, smiling.

"Grandpa!" Tar said, smiling.

"Hello, boys," Grandpa said.

Grandpa didn't look remotely like the spirit Dr. Dee and Edward Kelley questioned. He had on a navy-blue serge suit, the one he used to wear on Sundays, and carried a fancy cane. His shoes were highly polished underneath white spats. He looked the business, too, in an old-fashioned 1930s porn-star sort of way. "What can I do for you two boys?" he asked with characteristic directness. There was something on his lapel that looked suspiciously like soil.

"I'll do the talking," Tar hissed quickly. To their grandfather he said formally, "Grandpa, sir, there's been a family crisis."

"Nothing changes," Grandpa snorted cynically.

"It's Dad, sir," Tar pressed on. "His business has collapsed and he's lost nearly all our money."

"Your father was always an idiot," Grandpa sniffed. "Never knew why my daughter married him, except she's fairly dim as well." He brushed the loam off his lapel and glared at Tarquin. "What am I supposed to do about it?"

For some reason Tar felt embarrassed. He flushed slightly. "Mum said something about stock certificates. . . ." Actually Grandpa wasn't what he'd expected. Aside from the bed socks and the nightgown, the woman with Dr. Dee and Mr. Kelley *looked* like a spirit. She was all pale and transparent. But Grandpa wasn't. He looked real and solid and even smelled a bit. There was a glint in his eye Tar didn't like at all.

"So that's it!" Grandpa exclaimed, with the air of one on whom a light has dawned. "The little brat wants to get her greedy hands on my stock certificates!"

It was peculiar hearing your mother described as a "little brat," but Tar supposed you had to see things from her father's viewpoint. "Mum doesn't know we're doing this," he hastened to explain.

Grandpa wasn't listening. ". . . worked for every penny of my fortune," he was saying furiously, "and if she thinks she can swan off with it now and bail out that greasy cretin she married, she's got another think coming. Why do you imagine I never left a will?"

"But none of it's any use to you now," Tar protested. "You're dead!"

Grandpa grinned suddenly. "Not anymore," he said.

The magic circle was supposed to keep in anything you called up, but Grandpa walked out of it without a problem. He headed for the cellar steps, swinging his fancy cane.

"Quick," Tar hissed at Wit. "Read the License to Depart!"

Wit flicked the pages, found his place and intoned loudly, *"Ite in pace ad loca vestra et pax sit inter vos redituri ad mecum vos invocavero, in nomine Patris et Filii et Spiritus Sancti. Amen."* The Latin was supposed to get rid of anything up to and including Satan, but it didn't even slow Grandpa down. He clumped up the wooden staircase, jerked open the cellar door, and disappeared from view.

The twins stared after him.

"What are we going to do?" Wit asked at last.

"Let's go to bed and just pretend it never happened," Tar suggested.

Pretending didn't solve much. The next morning, their dad was still moaning on about the business, their mum was still desperate, and their grandfather . . . well, they didn't quite know what had happened to their grandfather. They talked about it on their way to school.

"You don't think he's . . . gone back?" Wit asked. "You know, to heaven or wherever?"

"I don't think he's gone anywhere," Tar told him. "I don't think he *liked* being dead." He caught his brother's expression and added, "Well, would you?"

"I don't know," Wit said. He thought about it and shook his head. "I don't suppose so." As they arrived at the gate—Beckham College, well-known and respected English public school for boys—he added, "Where do you think he's staying then?"

"It'll be the Carlton or the Ritz," said Tar. "They were always his favorite hotels." He hesitated. "Or maybe Blades." Blades was an exclusive club to which their grandfather had belonged. It didn't matter. With his money, Grandpa could afford to stay *anywhere.*

He could also afford to drive well, as the boys discovered later on that day. At Beckham, formal classes
ended at 4:30. The boarders were herded off to chapel,
but day boys caught buses, trains, cadged lifts, or what-
have-you, in order to get home. Since Tar and Wit lived
within walking distance of the college (and supper wasn't
until 7:30, when Dad got back from his broken business)
the twins often spent a little time in Ropo's, the new
coffee bar on Cardamon Street. Cassandra was already
there, already changed out of her school uniform,
already looking more like Britney than Britney did herself in a tiny denim skirt and top that showed off her
belly button ring.

"Coffee and a show?" asked Tar at once. There was
an early matinee at the Picture Palace.

"With me," suggested Wit smoothly, giving her the
smile. He might be slower off the mark, but when it came
to schmoozing women, he was far from stupid.

But Cass declined to play the usual game. "Sorry,"
she said. "I have a date." Then, because no girl who looks
like Britney can pass up a chance to rip your heart out,
she added, "With a real man, not a boy."

The twins retreated to a gloomy corner and ordered
coffee black, no sugar, for the bitter taste that suited their
mood. They watched Cassandra at her table, wondering
if she was telling the truth, until she jumped up suddenly
and swept past them in a cloud of smoking perfume.

They waited (but only just) until she pushed through the front door, then raced to press their noses to the window. Cassandra was climbing into the passenger seat of a brand-new, bright-red Lamborghini Muira. The car was driven by their grinning grandpa.

"He's old enough to be her father," Tar said, appalled.

"Her *grand*father," Wit corrected him, eyes wide and a little moist. It was a huge blow to their self-confidence. Cassandra had never dated either of them, but neither had she dated anybody else they knew.

Until now.

"But *why*?" Tar asked rhetorically. "Why *him* when it could have been *me*? Or even you," he added kindly.

"Money," Wit said cynically. "I'll bet he takes her to Jacob's on the Mall."

Jacob's on the Mall was one of several hundred excellent restaurants the boys could not afford.

"I'll bet he takes her back to his hotel," said Tar. "The Carlton or the Ritz. She'll be impressed. The concierge will smarm all over him. The doorman will call him by his name. They turn down the cover of your bed and leave you chocolates on the pillow."

"What are we going to do about it?" Wit asked, staring darkly into an uncertain future.

"Kill him," Tar said promptly.

"That's murder," Wit said.

"Not if he's already dead," Tar pointed out reasonably.

"But what if we get caught?"

"Doing what?" Tar asked rhetorically. "The most we could be charged with is interfering with a corpse."

All the same, they soon agreed it would be best to murder him discreetly. That way it avoided complications.

Grandpa was staying at the Ritz, just as Tar suspected. When the boys discovered he liked to dine at his hotel on nights he wasn't trying to seduce Cassandra, Wit wangled an evening job in the kitchens as dishwasher, mopper-upper, and general gofer. Tar found poison in the chemistry lab at school and stole enough to kill a horse.

The *soupe du jour* at the Ritz that evening was a spicy bouillabaisse the twins knew was one of Grandpa's favorites. The plan was for Wit to slip the poison into Grandpa's serving should he order it. The Ritz made a particularly fine bouillabaisse, rich in both texture and flavor and perfect to disguise any lingering taste of toxin.

As was the custom in most restaurants, Ritz waiters wrote their orders down, then left the dockets in the kitchens. Wit checked the docket from his grandfather's table and discovered the old boy had gone for the bouillabaisse exactly as they'd hoped. Wit hung around until a bowlful was ladled from the main tureen, then surreptitiously sprinkled in the poison.

"What eez it zat you are doing, kitchen boy?" a heavily accented voice inquired behind him. "Into ze zup you sprinkle somezing, *n'est-ce pas?*"

"Salt," Wit told the head chef promptly. He stared innocently into the florid face.

The head chef twirled the end of his mustache, then took a spoon and tasted the soup in the main tureen. "Sacred Blue!" he exclaimed. "You are right, kitchen boy. Ze bouillabaisse, she is underseasoned." He seized the poison packet from Wit's nerveless hand and dumped its contents into the tureen. Then he tasted again. *"Bon,"* he proclaimed. "Much better." He walked off, humming the "Marseillaise" to himself.

Wit watched through the service window as Grandpa drank his soup, but disappointingly the old boy failed to die.

"Must have been rubbish poison," Tar remarked afterward.

Wit shook his head. "No, they carted seven other patrons off to the hospital, and the Ritz is looking for a new head chef," he said. "It must be something to do with Grandpa."

"Maybe he's impossible to kill. Maybe you can't die twice," mused Tar.

It was an interesting theory and one they lost no time in putting to the test. Working after school and over the weekend, they embarked on a series of ingenious plans.

They stretched a trip wire on the stairwell of a parking garage and watched him fall down several flights of concrete steps. They sabotaged an elevator so that it plunged eighteen floors. They drained the brake fluid from his Lamborghini Muira. They drilled a hole in the bottom of a ferryboat. They dropped endless ornamental flowerpots from high buildings. They released a leopard from the zoo.

In each case Grandpa walked away from the ensuing carnage without so much as a bruise. The work on the Lamborghini Muira did have one unexpected side effect: after he wrote off the car, Cassandra wouldn't date him anymore.

"Very superficial values," Tar remarked.

"Perhaps we're better off without her," Wit suggested.

"Perhaps," Tar said.

It took a while, but they eventually realized that the business with Cassandra had changed things. They discussed it at some length after they were supposed to be asleep. The twins shared the same room, reclining one above the other in bunk beds.

"Why . . . ?" asked Wit hesitantly. "Why are we still trying to kill him?"

Tar waited for a moment then said, "Oh, I see what you mean. If Cassandra isn't going out with him now . . ."

"And we think we're better off without her . . ." Wit put in.

"Why should we waste our energy . . . ?" Tar said.

"Especially when Dad's nearly bankrupt . . ."

"And Mum's on pills for her nerves . . ."

"And we really should be doing something to help with family finances . . ."

They often talked like that, completing one another's sentences. It was part of being twins.

"Let's try Grandpa one more time," suggested Tar.

Wit blinked. "Try to kill him?"

"No, try to get some money out of him," Tar said.

Grandpa had taken a presidential suite at a cost (according to the brochure at reception) of two thousand pounds a night. He looked none the worse for all their murder attempts.

"Live fast, die young," he said with a grin, then called room service to bring them Cokes. "Now what can I do for you boys?"

"It's Dad . . ." Tar said.

"And Mum," Wit put in.

"And money," Grandpa added. "Boys, we've been down this road before."

"But that was before we knew you needed it," Tar said.

"I still need it," Grandpa said. "I'm heading for Bermuda this weekend."

"But you don't need *all* your money," Tar told him with emphasis. "Not even in Bermuda."

"What were you thinking of?" asked Grandpa.

"A small cash injection into Dad's business," Tar said. "Just to tide him over until the market rallies."

Room service arrived with Coca-Colas on a silver tray. The drinks had ice and lemon and some sort of fancy garnish. Grandpa stuffed a fifty into the waiter's pocket as a tip. "I see where you're coming from," he told the boys when the man had gone. "I really do. But after Bermuda, there's Las Vegas, then I plan to hit Monte Carlo and after that a world tour, maybe build a house in Surrey, find a woman my own age, and settle down. I was a long time dead."

"You owe us," Wit said suddenly.

Grandpa and Tar both turned to look at him.

"Well, you do!" Wit said. "You weren't a long time dead—it just seemed that way. But without us, you'd *still* be. Dead, I mean. Tar and me, we *resurrected* you."

There was a long, long silence in the room. Then Grandpa said, "You got a point there, Wit." He sipped his Coca-Cola. "Tell you what. I won't give you any of *my* money—goes against the grain too much—but I will tell you how to get some of your own. Maybe even a *lot* of your own."

Tar looked at Wit, then at his grandfather. "How?" he asked.

"Sell that book you used to call me back. Looked like a first edition from the glimpse I got. Could net you half a million from the right collector."

Half a million proved a little optimistic, but the twins cleared £415,000 after auction fees. They took the proceeds in cash, packed it into two small leather suit-cases, and splurged on a taxi to get them home. They passed Cassandra waiting at a bus stop. She had a new ring in her belly button.

". . . be enough to get Dad out of trouble?" Wit was saying.

Tar looked pensive. "Not sure we should give it to Dad now. Grandpa's right—he'll only waste it."

Wit looked at his brother in surprise. "What do you think we should do with it then?"

Tar glanced through the back window of the taxi. The lonely figure of Cassandra was still standing at the bus stop. "Thought we might buy ourselves a Lamborghini," he said.

No Visible Power

Deborah Noyes

From this time on the rooms were closely watched, and the strange, sinister effigies appeared every few days when no human being could have entered the room.

—*New Haven Journal*, Monday, April 22, 1892

We have not been in Stratford two weeks, and we have visitors.

The house, locked and solemn when we left for church this morning, has come to chaos. Our front door gapes. Shutters flap over windows black with holes. Glass glitters in the hydrangea bushes. "Back!" Father barks with upraised hand as we inch near in the Sunday silence.

"Have we been burgled?" Mama complains, sipping one of her tonics from a flask. She and my sister—fine specimens of the weaker sex—stand gaping, so I follow my father and brother inside, where doors wave open and cross breezes dance over a sea of smashed china and scattered fireplace tools, tipped chairs.

"No one's made off with the silver," Father hisses.

We must be still, it seems, for the quiet in the house is a sort of presence, easily offended.

"Fetch the others," he instructs, and young Tom bounds off while I follow up the stairs, the silky drag of my skirts the only sound.

"Who did this?" I whisper, prizing the pause in our routine—a routine as rigid in two weeks' time as it ever was up in Canada—but my father won't answer. He's reached the second story and stands transfixed outside the master bedroom.

The others arrive and crowd behind us.

Lying in there, stiff across the bed in Father's clothes, is a figure. Or, more to it, lying like a figure are Father's clothes. Someone has taken care to primp and arrange the stuffed impostor, from wing collar and vest to frock coat and watch chain. The arms are crossed, like a body arranged for burial. Mama fans herself with great force while Amelia simpers. Father commences clawing through the Bible on his nightstand. Tom and I just stand there. Only our maid, arriving late to the scene, has sense enough to dismantle the doll with one swipe of her arm. Clacking her tongue, Harvey waves us out so she can reclaim us, room by room.

For weeks now I've tried in vain to remember our lives in Saskatchewan, where we lived before. On this night, however—and every haunted night succeeding it—the dam of memory opens a little. When the gong of the grandfather clock wakes me, I watch myself as in a dream, with composed detachment, and I am home on the plains again, marching alongside the village idiot in his cart:

Milt's head is bald and glossy when he lifts the shapeless hat in greeting. He smiles at the reins and, for a long while, just bumps along beside me.

Father and I quarreled horribly the night before about my "rights" or lack thereof, and at dawn, my drowsy fury gave way to despair. I packed a bag and crept across creaking floorboards. The prairie at that hour was steeped in gold, and my pinched heart expanded to see it.

But I am as good as hollow from last night's weeping. The wind has since picked up, coursing in me like the breath in a flute, whipping loose strands of my hair. My pointy-toed boots cut my flesh, and my hand, closed over the handle of a carpetbag, is painfully dry. I wish I'd filched some of Amelia's fussy lavender oil, though I wouldn't have thought to need such frills where I'm going, to beg my spinster aunt in Regina for shelter.

And then I glimpse the tents outside town, a kingdom of promise on the far horizon. I remember what Harvey whispered under her breath a few days earlier, when we rattled past in Father's coach. Her conspiring breath had tickled my ear. "I heard it was here, Mary—not a stone's throw away—Bill Cody's Wild West Show!"

Father would tolerate no such frivolity, of course, but

it occurs to me now, striding under Milt's shy gaze, that Buffalo Bill might take me in. And why not? I'm a quick study, Harvey says. Aunt Georgie says it, too. Buffalo Bill could teach me to rope and ride and blast-three-times-my-Stetson like Little Sure Shot, Annie Oakley. He could make my dreams come true.

As I march, my patient neighbor bumps along in the wagon, his horse blowing frosty blasts through her nostrils, tail flicking. Milt is serene as can be, a gentle presence, and the cries of the arrowing geese overhead give me hope. That's a good noise, I think, a sweet sight. It reminds me the world is large, larger than Father would have me know.

"They shall enter in at all the windows like thieves," my parent booms at breakfast the next morning. Father cleans and oils his pistol with care while we peer over teacups. He cannot resist his Bible. He claims we came all this way to Stratford to escape it—the barren northwest plains, but his calling, too. "For a time," Mama confided mysteriously in Aunt Georgie as we packed our trunks, hinting at grief and a grave and grown-up woes beyond my knowing, "he doubted his faith. Now it is restored, but he has no heart to preach."

Father is a retiring Presbyterian minister, he jokes to anyone who'll listen, including strangers on the train that delivered us here, and we avert our eyes. "Retiring" he is not.

* * *

In the days to come, other strange, stuffed figures appear. It's a wonder we have a scrap of cloth left in this house to cover our poor bodies with, so many garments have been shred and shaped to spectral play.

The pace of our haunting has picked up in other ways, too. Umbrellas sail through the air. Keys, knives, and nails fall from locations from which no person could have released them. Underclothes rain down in a gleeful, humiliating display, floating like feathers, landing lightly. Turnips turn up with splendid regularity, and today at lunch a potato plopped into Tom's soup, splashing him soundly. Several times daily, the knocker beats a rhythm on the front door. Father or Harvey races there and flings it open only to find an empty porch. Increasingly though, when the knocker sounds, a caller *is* there. Curiosity seekers come in hoards now: new acquaintances, reporters, investigators.

Daily, Amelia narrates our plight, reading aloud at breakfast from the *Journal* in mock-ominous tones: "'These effigies were fashioned and arranged, this observer believes"—she glances up as she recites, greeting each gaze in turn—"by no *visible* power.'"

Our sorrows have made my sister a celebrity outside our walls, which status she savors, I think. The party atmosphere here delights her. Mother, too. Harvey, for her part, must empty spittoons and keep up with crumbs. Father's graying old school friends are ever eager for refreshment. Today one of these distinguished gentlemen suggests the whole muddle is *our* doing. "It's the children, I wager, or the maid behind it."

I brace myself for Father's reply, and sure enough he greets the challenge with good cheer, striding to the closet in the facing hall. He opens the door, which gapes like a mouth. "Children?" he croons. "Harvey . . . you'll do the honors. We must prove ourselves blameless, it seems."

Mama begs, "Elisha," in a tone sweetly exasperated, but her nerves betray her. She cannot wave her fan fiercely enough, realizing too late that she has drawn attention to herself.

"And you as well, Margaret. If you will."

Mama turns a hideous shade of scarlet as the assembled, a blur of pipe smoke and sideburns, smile and murmur among themselves.

As Father herds us into the dark, his eyes shine with sport. "Take a candle," he adds kindly, when someone troubles to light one.

No sooner has he slapped the door shut than the flame blows out. We huddle close to Harvey since Mama, whimpering and repellent, is cold comfort. Amelia soon erupts in fear and hysteria. "It's touching me!" my sister cries, slapping at herself. "I am pinched!" Harvey holds her but to little avail, and in frustration I shrink back into a corner. Gradually—though my sister snivels and hiccups—her cries cease, and we are no more accosted.

When a bookshelf sees fit to crash to the floor out front, Father releases us.

It is all any of us can do after that to look at him, smug and triumphant, or at his cronies with their brandy and learned banter: light and energy and the secret lives of objects.

When I stop marching, Milt halts the wagon, too, though he doesn't offer a hand to help me up, doesn't lean and say, "Need a lift, little lady?" as any other country neighbor might do, basking in manly anonymity and the chance to sit by a full-figured girl with carpetbag and tear-streaked face. To be of use.

I make my own way up, tossing the bag in first.

Milt's a simpleton, they say. He's not mute but may as well be. He's like furniture or the old signs that point you out of town, reliably present, yet not. Unlike other townsmen—Mr. So-and-So or Dr. or sir—he's always been Milt, just Milt, and it's proper to address him so. Maybe no one remembers his surname. Maybe, like Buffalo Bill, he needs no other name. Maybe he doesn't have one.

An odd old sea captain built this house. He died not long before we arrived. I suspect this haunting is all his doing: an eccentricity, like his glossy twin staircases. These meet at the second-floor landing to ape the lay of a clipper ship. The whole house is a shadowy sprawl, thick with history, crawl spaces, and intricate carved moldings.

The captain's house is unlike our former home, a squat farmstead on the prairie, in every way. The very landscape here seems opposed to us. Connecticut born and bred, Father may be at home, but we others distrust the clutter of grand homes and trees, boats bobbing at the edge of a vast, immoderate ocean. The rest of us come from a place of modest plank-and-shingle dwellings and endless sky. You hide nothing under such a sky.

When visitors are scarce, as they are this morning, a pall blankets the house. Well I know that God hates an idle hand, so I root out an embroidery sampler from the basket by the mahogany tea table. Before our specters came, needlework—chief among womanly arts—was the core of my and Amelia's accursed education. I loathe this task above all others, but today its tedium soothes me. I stitch and stitch, dutiful as dishwater. I stitch GO AWAY, a message for these meddlesome ghosts. A spirit telegram, if you will.

When Mama later finds my handiwork on the chair, her eyes shine with horror. *"Go?"* she scoffs, backing away. "Where would they have us go?"

"They are the ones . . ." I stammer from the doorway, trying to soothe her. *"They* must go."

She only utters an impatient sob, sweeping the sampler onto the floor as if it were a silverfish, and I confess this surprises me: I rate it among my better work.

"This is our home," Mama whispers, but her eyes are dull. Her voice lacks conviction. It pains me to see her this way, though she herself has purchased our sorrows with her endless agreement, her tonics and weepiness. She has not strength to forbid them entry, whoever they are.

"Isn't she a vision?" Mother asks nervously, fanning herself. Her sole aim is to maintain normality where none remains. "Amelia has a suitor coming tonight, you'll recall."

Father grumbles behind his broadsheet, and there is a collective intake of breath until he lays it down. Amelia shimmers in one of Mama's old satin ball gowns, altered to her full figure, the bodice swooping to suit the fashion. There's a big impertinent bustle in back.

Silent a long while, Father folds the paper, creasing it with utmost care to match his creased forehead. His jaw is set under his sideburns, and he lays his hands flat, staring them down. "I might praise your gown, Amelia . . . could I find it."

With that, his hands seize the water pitcher, flinging its contents full at her. It's my sister he douses, but I flinch, too, from habit. Father sets the pitcher down and massages his eyelids with his thumbs. "But there is too little dress to speak of, and less still of modesty. Let me not look on this *vision* again," he complains. "Leave me."

Amelia obeys, wet through and shivering, choking back tears, I trust (for who understands better than I the vain struggle to win Father's approval?). Hearing her light step on the stair, our aggrieved parent beseeches the heavens, "Why I was cursed with such willful and reckless daughters is beyond my comprehension." Harvey follows Amelia out, and Father roars after them, "I am *sick* with it." He rests his perspiring forehead on the tabletop.

Mama tries to stroke his hair, but he beats his sorry skull against the wood in protest. *"Sick, sick, sick,"* he chants. My mother clears her throat primly, and, with Harvey in rebellion, steels herself to clear the dishes.

Water, water . . . everywhere. We carry bucketfuls, day and night now (putting me in mind of our captain again, though I taste no salt in this latest tide of trouble. I taste little these days, and I sleep even less). Water streams down the walls. It puddles in the seats of chairs, soaks the contents of dresser drawers, and seeps through the very floorboards. Mattresses and cushions get so wet they have to be stripped and set outside to air. We mop and sponge in vain, for there is no rain and nothing leaking. The well is as it was. It is like trying to bail out the old rowboat Harvey and Tom and I stowed in a tangle of raspberry bushes by the river near our old farm. Water rises in the glassware and dishes. One day, when Father sent for some ripened cherries, the bowl

Harvey carried filled to the brim with pink water, over-
flowing at his feet. Our basement is ever full, and when
I dip my foot in, the water is cold. The water is raging.

*For a while Milt and I ride along, companionably silent,
but his smile, childlike and knowing, begins to vex me.
Surveying the tents on the flat horizon, bright against a
monotonous blue sky, I ask, "Which way you going at the
crossroads, Milt?"*

He motions west.

*"All the way to Regina?" For this is where I mean to
go, too, to find my aunt. Like Harvey, Georgie has ever
treated what Father calls my "willful" idiosyncrasies with
tolerance and sympathy. She'll take me in.*

*Milt's eyebrows, a pucker of embarrassment, tell me,
yes, he's going to Regina, and yes, he'll see me safely . . .*

*"All right, Milt. What are you smiling about?" You can
talk to him that way—straight on—as you can't other
adults. This is why, when I chance to think of him at all,
I like him. "What's so funny?"*

*He shrugs, red all the way to his ears. His white hands
with their black and bitten nails hold the worn leather
reins at some distance, as if they're precious.*

*"You won't say you saw me today. With this"—I hold
up my carpetbag—"will you, Milt? You won't give Father
the satisfaction of knowing which way I went."*

He is silent, his lips pinched, smiling.

"Thank you, Milt."

* * *

Why we stay, I cannot fathom. Always now, there are screams and indistinct voices. The ghosts rap and they pound. Mama's nerves are very bad. Glass and pottery burst, and spoons hover or wilt in midair. Windows shatter, and Father orders them replaced. It is a contest of wills to his mind, and stubborn as these ghosts may be, he will win. I cannot doubt it.

Still, marble-topped tables rear up like horses. It is lovely sometimes, hypnotic, these objects in their unlikely arrangements in space. I feel myself lulled, transfixed by it, but more and more now—as if to spite my calm—there is violence, too. A sturdy brass candlestick might jump off the mantel and pound itself against the floor to breaking. Once when Father and Amelia went out driving, they were barraged with stones, counting twenty on the carriage floor. Few stay long in our home now, except to gawp or gossip for the broadsheets, and on another afternoon, a note fluttered down during one of Mama's now desperately underattended tea parties: "Beelzebub begs the ladies to accept as proof of his favor this compliment." And the teapot cracked like an egg, its contents staining the tablecloth the shade of dried blood.

This morning, when the others go about their errands, Father and I stand watch as usual, though as usual I keep out of sight. How strange it is to sit so silently by him, to hear his shallow breathing. I suspect my father's heart beats fiercely, and for a moment, in this unlikely posture of fellowship, I almost understand him. He cares for us, above all, but his care is single-minded. It is exacting. Sweat beads up on his brow, and he frowns so horribly I am almost afraid of him. When he loops round to patrol the front rooms again, I follow without a peep.

We are used to surprises, but today in the dining room we find a whole crowd of women, posed for religious devotion. Some bow so low their foreheads touch the floor. Each is utterly still, in worship. And what do they worship? A demonic thing suspended from a cord in the center of the room. Suppose you dried, like meat jerky, a birdlike, infant gnome—this is what you'd have. Our effigy is the brown of earwax, bent-winged, and hideously distorted, with the barest suggestion of a face.

Fashioned from scraps—old blankets, muffs, clothing (some not yet unpacked since our arrival)—the worshippers are so lifelike, we don't at once realize they are dummies, as Father Death in the master bedroom was, and the others since.

Who devised this grim tableau? It would take an army of seamstresses and hours of steady labor to assemble it. Father moves nimbly among the stuffed flock, pausing to peer at an open Bible on the floor. His forefinger tracing the marked page, he reads aloud: "When you pass through the waters, I will be with you; and through the rivers, they shall not overflow you. . . ." His

voice trails off. He looks furtively round, as if to catch
the culprit or culprits, as if they might be breathing down
his neck. It is a passage from Isaiah, and for a moment it
seems my stern father, the noble Reverend Elisha David
Dowell, will weep in fear and consternation. But the
moment passes—too soon. He straightens his tie. He
resolves to tear them down.

Retiring after dinner to the sitting room, we children
find a lone figure in Father's reading chair. It wears the
blue satin sash from Amelia's scandalous dress tied, like
a gag, where its mouth would be. Tom looks especially
horrified and perplexed. "Mary doesn't even like dolls,"
he blurts, inexplicably. Amelia and I regard him with
sad disapproval. I may *feel* helpless as a child these days,
but I'm fifteen and far too old for dolls, even if I did favor them, which I don't.

"Tom!" I turn to my sister's voice, relieved that
someone has broken the unbearable silence, but then
she rushes at Tom, shaking his shoulders, rattling the
poor child silly. "She's gone!" Amelia's gesture takes in
everything, the whole house. "*Let* her go . . ."

We are beset! I would remind them. Instead I race to
the dummy in Father's chair and yank Amelia's sash off,
using it to catch my naughty brother by his neck, lasso
him as Annie Oakley might do, as we children might
have done in play before our sorrows came. I lead him
like a leashed dog (one that has planted its paws firmly

and won't budge) back into the windowless pantry closet where we store firewood. I pull the door closed as Amelia, shrieking hysterically, commands me to give him back. She kicks the wood, but I know she won't venture in. Since Father shut us in the closet to conduct his experiment, Amelia has developed an unnatural fear of enclosed spaces. Now she begins to call for him, though we all know he has gone out for his evening walk. The same walk on the same path at the same hour every night.

How black it is. I clutch and whisper into my little brother's hair—ivory-soft as milkweed down, I know, though I can't feel it, though he complains and stamps and shakes. Poor Tom. I kiss his cheek to calm him, rock with his rocking, and try to taste the salt of his tears, but taste nothing. I try to feel the warmth I know is there in his skin and feel nothing. I try to shed the tears that threaten to burst me and cannot, though the walls are streaming with them. How frightened we both are. How damp the closet is. I know it's my fault, all my fault, yet I don't know how to change it. We're huddled together, he hiccupping and out of breath from sobbing, me limp and exhausted from wishing it away, all away, when a flood of light sweeps over us.

The shock in Mother's eyes, to see him in my arms with that sash round his neck, is savage. She plucks her precious sobbing son from the closet, and I feel the silk slide through my fingers. Mama slaps the door shut, and I am alone. I am forsaken, and for a moment—the longest

moment of my short life, with my head roaring—I hover
in the quiet dark. I suffer the temptation of it.

When at last I venture out alone, they've gone, but
Mama has fetched my embroidery sampler and propped
it in the doorwell.

GO AWAY, it reads.

I lift it as Amelia appears on the threshold. Her eyes
seem fixed on the sampler, and I hear her whisper, "Mary?"

Harvey enters, too, grasping Amelia's quivering shoulders. "*Dear* Mary," she says, nodding hard at nothing.
"You must go now."

I fling the sampler, and their vague eyes follow it. I
touch my cheek lightly, so lightly. Elbow. Eyelid. Throat.
How sweet it would be to sleep, even without a good-
night kiss—for none in this stuffy house, it seems, will
grant me even that. They would sooner forget me.

*"Are you simple, Milt?" I lick my chapped lips. It has
dawned on me that Milt's idiocy is like a veil, concealing
him from a world that will not have him as he is, will not
take him whole. "Are you* really*?"*

He nods his dreamy, relentless smile.

*My aunt will shelter me, I know, but I know, too, that
the nature of plans is sudden. That's what Harvey always
whispered as we pored by candlelight—safe from Father's
prohibitions—over dime novels, love poems, and the lurid
stories in ladies' magazines; there is no other way for a
woman to navigate, except by instinct.*

What I do next dims my companion's smile a little, but I'll leave him with a parting gift. "I've changed my mind, Milt, about going to Regina. Watch this—" And I leap off the moving wagon, tumbling into the gulch. I roll to my feet like a spry demon, a dazzling apparition. "I'm alive"—I pluck my carpetbag from the field, a rush of manure filling my nostrils, and my voice scatters like a flock of birds into the wind—"and I'm flying!"

For a moment, before Buffalo Bill's Wild West—that faraway city of tents across the river—takes my full attention, I see myself, the back of myself, as Milt saw me: bounding, muddy-kneed, my coffee-colored curls flapping loose from their pins.

Good-bye.

Galloping with nettle-scarred gown flapping behind like a sail, I'm the girl that got away. Milt's hearty laughter, full throated—a man's laughter or an angel's, not a child's or an idiot's—surprises me, and I understand that the promise of this moment is why he'd been smiling in the first place.

But now, to get to the bright tents beyond, I have to cross the swollen river, and I realize too late that the raging water will weigh me down and take me. How much I've wanted to be free, like Annie Oakley and the arrowing geese. It is all I've ever wanted, and now I shall be.

Bad Things

Libba Bray

It was Brian's idea to go devil worshipping. The newspaper had reported the story all week: out on Route 211, past the cemetery, they'd found the mutilated cattle, all of them cut wide open in a ritual fashion. Rumors raced through the town like a flash flood. The cow's hearts were all missing. No, it was the guts—they'd been arranged in the grass as an offering to the Dark Prince himself. Small fires had been left burning. Several crosses were desecrated. A design had been chalked into the grass. Was it a pentagram? Yes. It was definitely a pentagram, or so said a girl who knew the cousin of somebody whose uncle was a state trooper. The details didn't matter so much, because everyone agreed: Satanists had come to Damascus, Texas, population 15,401. Hiding among us— maybe in the hardware store or a parking space at the

Sonic, at the Baptist potlucks, the drive-in movies, or on the metal bleachers of our dusty football stadium— were diabolical people. Mutilators. Killers. Devil worshippers. The town gave off a perfume of fearful excitement. My friends and I were alive with the kind of terrible joy you feel when the sky bruises over and the wind picks up before a storm with the threat of a tornado that also feels like a promise. A feeling like finally something's coming that you can't avoid, that you can face head-on, and in that stand, you'll either be made or lost forever.

"So, what should we do first when we catch the Satanists?" Brian asked, his blue Dodge Dart inching its way down the busy Saturday-night strip. We passed a few carloads of seniors out cruising, looking for early graduation parties. As juniors, we still had another year to go.

I shrugged and took a sip off my wine cooler. It tasted like Kool-Aid gone bad. "Dude, we're not gonna see any Satanists. It's probably just some hoax."

"You don't know that," Jimmy said, playing with the shark's tooth he wore on a chain around his neck. He smiled big. "I hear they *ate* the hearts, man. They have to do that to prove their loyalty to the devil. Cattle hearts are okay, but it's a human heart that really seals the deal."

"Ew, gross," Marla said. She was wearing some guitar-pick earrings that she thought made her look rocker-chick tough. "How do you fight a devil worshipper anyway? I mean, like, a crazy person? You can run away or kill them or, you know, like, outsmart them. But if they've got the devil on their side, how can you fight that?"

There's no such thing as a fair fight. The words popped into my head and stuck there. I'd said it to Hank once. But I didn't want to think about that now.

A red truck jacked up on huge wheels gunned its engine beside the Dodge. The redneck stuck his head out the window and took a good look at us—the guys long-haired and sloppy, the girls with bleached-out hair and too much eye makeup. Without thinking, I crossed my arms over my Led Zeppelin T-shirt and slunk down in the seat, trying to erase all traces of myself—the long skinny legs, my bony knees poking through the holes in my jeans, the lone earring in my left ear, the brown hair cut spiky short on top and longer in the back just like these British rockers I'd seen on the cover of *Creem* magazine, acne on my jaw that I was trying to hide with two days of barely there blond stubble. The redneck spit down a wad of chewing tobacco. It landed on the passenger door. "Freaks."

Jimmy leaned across K.J. and me and stuck his head out the back window. "Careful, man. We might be devil worshippers." He made the sign of horns with his fingers and flicked his tongue.

"You're a bunch of freaks and sluts," the redneck spat back. The light changed to green, and he was off in a cloud of dust.

"Aren't you going to chase him?" Jimmy asked as the truck's taillights glowed red and angry in the distance.

Brian angled the Dodge off the strip. "Naw, man. We've got a date with some cow mutilators."

We drove for miles over bumpy roads, past lonely houses and ranches that got to be spaced farther and farther apart. This was complete Nowheresville. Nothing but mesquite and cottonwood trees, scrub and the occasional cow or goat. Just past Route 211, the car's high beams swept over the iron gates of Rosethorn graveyard. Headstone angels and marble crosses poked into the thin high shafts of the Dodge's headlights in slashes of angry white, like things of the dark that were angry to be nudged awake and pulled into the light.

"This place creeps me out," K.J. said. "You think they could be in here somewhere?" She slunk down in her seat, peering out at the mausoleums rising up like crooked teeth. "I mean, how would you know what they even look like?"

Jimmy snickered. "They're the ones in shirts that say, I heart Beelzebub." K.J. giggled at his lame joke and Jimmy took it as encouragement. "You can worship Satan—ask me how!"

Marla reached over the front seat and grabbed a can of beer from the floorboard. "They wouldn't be here. It's hallowed ground." She popped the top and took a sip.

"Know a lot about it, Marla?" Brian said, goading her.

She rolled her eyes and flipped her straight black hair over her shoulders. "Not personally. But I've read stuff. Seen movies. They always find out later that the haunted house was built on an ancient burial ground or witch-burning mound or something like that." I watched her take another sip off the beer. Her mouth was wet and glossy.

"You know what's creepy? I read this book on numerology?" K.J. said. All her statements sounded like questions. "And it said that elevens and twos are, like, really unstable numbers? Because you can't divide anything into them, or something. I don't know. But they're, like, supposed to have some super-heavy vibe attached to them. Don't you think that's kind of weird? That this is Route 211?"

Jimmy put his arm around her. "Don't worry. I'll protect you." He'd had the hots for her since seventh-grade gym class when she told him she liked his free-throw shot. It didn't take much for Jimmy.

K.J. shrugged him off and I was secretly glad, not because I wanted to date K.J. myself, but because at least I wouldn't be the odd man out if Brian and Marla hooked up, which it seemed like they might.

"But seriously, isn't that kind of weird? Like, when you think about it, a lot of bad stuff has happened on this road. Like, there was that car accident a few years ago on graduation night? All those seniors died?"

Jimmy snorted. "They were completely wasted, like an after-school special waiting to happen."

"AND there was that fire in the old barn ten years ago that killed a bunch of workers. They couldn't figure out how it started."

Brian took a swig off Marla's beer. "They did find out. It was a faulty generator."

K.J. was getting steamed that no one was buying her evil-road theory. "Well, I just think it's weird, that's all."

Jimmy pawed at her. "Lions and tigers and serial killers, oh my!"

K.J. slapped his arm. "Shut up, Jimmy," she whispered.

The car got still. No one looked at me. I hated that more than anything. The pity.

"Forgot my cancer sticks. Marla, can I have a drag?" I grabbed the menthol out of her fingers and took a big puff, wincing at the sweet mint taste of it. I exhaled, and the smoke hung in the air like a ghost.

"Sorry, man." Jimmy said quietly.

"It's okay." That's what they needed me to say, so I did.

"If they'd caught that guy, I would have thrown the switch myself," Marla said, taking out another smoke.

"Me, too," Brian echoed.

"He'll get his someday, that's for sure," Jimmy said, and K.J. nodded.

People had a way of saying things like that to me: "He'll get his." "God will find a way." "Justice will be served." I guess they thought it made me feel better about everything that happened, but it didn't. It only made them feel better. The truth was, there was no justice. They didn't catch the guy. For all I knew, he could be living it up in Dallas never once thinking about what he did. Evil had blown through town and it didn't even leave a name.

I remember the way Hank looked at Morrison's Funeral Home, laid out in a neat black suit inside the small cherrywood coffin with the red silk lining, paid for by some church group. His brown hair had been cut and oiled into place, his hands placed across his chest.

Lots of people had turned out. The place was packed with mourners. Everybody wanted to see the kid that had been taken from us and torn up. There were rumors about everything the guy had done to Hank, stuff I didn't even want to think about much less hear whispered in the hallways. While the ladies in their church dresses brought my mother endless cups of coffee and the men took my dad out back to smoke cigarettes in silence, I decided to go back to the viewing room. I needed to see Hank one last time, to tell him I was sorry for something I'd said that morning.

The room was quiet except for the hum of the air conditioner and the murmured sounds of crying and comforting that were coming from the other rooms. It was just me and Hank. I knelt on the soft red carpet and put my hands on the cold wood of the casket, drawing close till I was looking right at my dead brother, at his pale skin, the heavy makeup where Mr. Morrison had done his best to cover up the bruises, the violence, the coroner's stitching.

"I'm sorry, Hank," I whispered. Everything I'd been holding back rose up like a rain-swollen creek washing over the banks of me. "I didn't mean it, buddy. I'm sorry. I'm sorry," I croaked out between big snotty sobs. I let my arms stretch across his body and pressed my face into the side of the coffin, crying till I couldn't cry any more, till my eyelids were too heavy to bear their own weight and I had to close them.

I guess that's when I fell asleep and had the dream. At least, that's what the doctor told my parents later. A night terror, he called it. The kind of badass dream that's so intense and real it feels like you're really awake, that it's really happening.

I don't know about that. All I know is that while I was kneeling there with my arms out, I felt Hank move under them. Just a little—enough to make me sit back on my heels. That's when I saw Hank's eyelids snap wide open. Under the shades of them, his eyes were black and wet as fresh tar. I couldn't move, couldn't do anything. My little brother opened his mouth, the mortician's thread popping as he did, and it was black in there, too, like he'd been eating licorice and saving up the juice to gross me out. He sat straight up then.

"Danny . . ." he whispered in a voice that sounded wet and strangled. "There are bad things, Danny. Things you don't know about. But *they* know about *you*."

His hand touched my arm and, oh God, it was cold, colder than anything I'd ever felt, and still I didn't move, not until he gave me a smile that was straight out of hell, the black goo dribbling out the sides of his mouth and all those sharp points of teeth showing.

They say I screamed a scream that would trap the blood inside your veins. I screamed until people came running and found me kicking at Hank's coffin till it overturned and his body lay on the carpet, dead and quiet. My mom cried and my dad got that tight edge to his jaw. He was ready to beat me and I would have been grateful for it at that point, grateful for some kind of sharp pain that felt normal and made me stop seeing Hank's creepy black eyes, stop hearing his syrupy voice telling me the bad things had their eye on me. But one of the church ladies stepped in and pulled Dad away.

"He's been through a lot, too, Murphy," she said. "Take him home now. He just needs to rest."

But I didn't rest. I haven't rested much since. In my dreams, I feel myself frozen in place, being pushed toward that high burnished coffin. I see my brother's too-white hands gripping the sides of it. I see him push his body up and out. I see the papery skin covering his bony chest, see the pulsing heart thumping up against it like a fist beating at a door to be let in where it's safe and warm, away from those bad men with quick smiles and dead eyes and offers of candy in exchange for a little ride that never ends. I see my brother open his mouth, see that thick black ooze, those sharp points of his teeth glinting in the moonlight, freezing the scream in my throat.

"Here we are. Devil-worship central," Brian said, turning off the engine. We were at the edge of some green fields. People had been coming by, leaving bouquets of flowers wrapped up in plastic like offerings meant to get them close to the action and keep them safe at the same time, little tokens to show whatever god was out there that they were *good* people, people who should be *spared*, people who believed in a *fair fight*. The flowers were mostly trampled and dead now, and the people all gone. We were the only ones out there. Just us and the devil worshippers.

Brian flipped off the Dodge's headlights, and the place fell into a blackness you forget exists when you live in town. The kind that reminds you that civilization is still pretty new and that beyond the malls, churches, and post offices, the barbershops with free giveaway mugs, there is a deep, unrelenting dark that never goes away.

"Hey," Marla said. "Keep the lights on, okay?"

"I hear nine out of ten devil worshippers are at-tracted to car headlights," Jimmy joked. But Brian put the lights on anyway.

Marla pulled out the booze and we sat in the road to wait. We were primed for danger, ready to meet evil head-on instead of feeling it in the sneaky sucker-punch ways it had been dogging us most of our lives: moms running off in the middle of the night with guys they met in A.A. meetings; pink slips that made dads drink themselves into a stupor if we were lucky and into a rage if we weren't; the dead-end jobs and craphole apartments waiting for us once we got our diplomas; little brothers disappearing on a clear summer afternoon outside the Circle K. The bike still left on its side around back. The mom so beaten down by everything she couldn't even let herself hold on to any kind of hope when the cops showed up, so she stood there with a hand on her stomach, like maybe she could catch the bad luck of us there in her fist and throw it away once and for all.

Yeah, we were primed for a fight with an enemy we could see and feel and taste. No more sucker punches. We were ready to prove to ourselves that we could look the devil in the eye and survive. We were going to change our luck.

"Hey, guys? What's that?" Jimmy sounded freaked-out. He peered down into the tall grass. "Oh God . . . what is that?"

K.J. looked ready to cry. "Jimmy, stop it. You're creeping me out."

"There's something in the grass. Oh Jesus! Oh my God, it's a . . . HEART!"

Marla and K.J. screamed as Jimmy threw something wet and bloody at them. Brian yelped and fell back on his butt. The thing that had been in Jimmy's hand landed in the grass with a wet thunk. Shaking, I shone my flashlight on the ground where it had fallen, shiny, slick with blood, like something just born.

Jimmy doubled over laughing. "Oh, man! I wish I'd had a camera!"

"What the hell did you just throw at us, Jimmy!" K.J. demanded.

Jimmy was laughing so hard he was practically crying. "Chicken livers. Been planning that one all night. God, your face!"

K.J. pummeled Jimmy. "That was not funny, Jimmy!" But she started laughing while she hit him. He took her fists in his hands, and it was obvious to any idiot there they'd be making out before the night was over.

"I scared you good, man." Jimmy laughed.

Someday I'll make you scared of me. Just you wait.

Marla brushed my arm. "Danny, you okay? You sick?"

I shook my head. "Nah, I'm cool."

"Ohhh, dude! Admit it—I freaked your ass out!"

"Shut up, Jimmy!" Marla said.

But he didn't. "Hey, everybody, turns out Danny is really a girl!" He laughed hard, just like I'd done to Hank that time.

"Yeah," I said quietly. "That must be it."

* * *

The morning my little brother disappeared, he was driving me crazy. I was trying to put some new speakers into my crappy Honda and I needed to concentrate. But he just wouldn't shut up. It was stupid shit, too. Eight-year-old-boy shit, like what if Peter Parker was allergic to the spider who bit him? Can Superman do it to Lois Lane without killing her? Why doesn't Batman have any super-powers? That kind of stuff. I would've done anything to get rid of him.

"Hey, Danny?" Hank crawled into the passenger seat. I had my head under the steering wheel, messing with red and blue wires that didn't make sense to me yet.

"What?"

"You think Green Goblin could take Batman in a fair fight?"

"No such thing as a fair fight."

"Just answer the question. For real this time."

"I did."

His foot slipped, clocking me on the ear. I flinched and banged my head on the bottom of the dash.

"Dammit, Hank!"

His eyes got big. I must have looked like Dad on a bender. "Sorry, Danny."

"Yeah, you are sorry. A sorry-assed, good-for-nothing sissy! Why don't you ride bikes with your girlfriends," I snarled.

"We're not girls."

"Coulda fooled me."

"Stop it! You . . . just stop it!" His face crunched up, like he was going to cry. It made me brave with cruelty. I could have stopped. I should have. But there was something about having all that power over him. Something about winning for once in my life, even if it was winning at something so petty, that took over. I wanted to crush him. To be the last one standing.

"I'll bet you think about doing it with guys all the time, don't you, Hank? I'll bet you and your girlfriends are all a bunch of homos."

He took a swing at me and I knocked him back on his butt. And then he did start to cry. I'd won. But it hadn't been a fair fight. Not by a long shot. And the excitement I'd felt earlier had gone away, leaving me irritated and disgusted—with myself for being such a jerk and with him for taking it. Suddenly, I couldn't get rid of him fast enough. I just wanted him gone.

"Forget you, Danny!" he yelled, wiping snot on his sleeve.

"Oooh, I'm scared." I hid my head under the steering wheel again.

"Someday I'll make you scared of me! Just you wait!"

I heard the crunch of his tires on the gravel, the whip of his Hot Wheels pennant flapping in the wind. And that's the last memory I have of my brother alive.

"*Shhh*," Brian said. "Shut up. I hear something."

Jimmy let out a little snort. "Nice try, Johnson."

"No. For real." Brian shut off the music. He seemed nervous and awake, the way he used to look up at bat when we were in junior high, before his dad went on disability and Brian had to quit the team. "There!" he said quickly. "You hear that?"

There was a low, deep sound coming from the trees. Could have been cattle. Maybe.

"Come on," Brian whispered. "I think they're here."

"Maybe we should get out of here," Marla said, taking K.J.'s hand.

But Brian took my flashlight, flipped it on, and was heading for the trees. "No, man. Let's go check it out. I'm not leaving till I bag me a Satanist."

We crept through the trees behind Brian and the light. Marla grabbed my hand and squeezed. Any other time, I'd be thinking of where it would lead, but now I was only thinking about that sound getting louder. It made my stomach tighten with a weird mix of fear and excitement. This was how it felt to be alive. Kill or be killed. It couldn't be simpler.

We pushed on, and the trees closed around us more and more, until the car's headlights were just a distant, faint sheen. The noise was close now, close enough that I could tell it wasn't moaning. It was some kind of chanting. The sound traveled up my spine and lay strong fingers around the back of my neck.

"Dude," I whispered. "Hear that?"

Brian held the light under his chin and nodded. His

face glowed as white as one of the marble angels in the cemetery. He was smiling big. "Devil worshipping is now in session."

K.J. stopped short, hugging herself. "I wanna go home."

"I'll protect you," Jimmy said, putting his arms around her like the total horn dog he was.

We'd reached the edge of the trees and pushed out into the wide clearing where the cows had been found. Sun-bleached wooden crosses put out by the locals stood like a bunch of scarecrows. I couldn't tell where the chanting was coming from. It seemed like it came from all around us. And just like that, it stopped.

"Okay, that's officially weird," Marla whispered. Her hand was sweaty in mine.

"Forget it. I'm going back," K.J. said, pulling at Jimmy's lanky arm.

A high-pitched scream split the air. It made my whole body go tight with a buzzing like bees under my skin. And then it came again—a horrible howl like someone being gutted alive.

K.J. started crying. "Oh my God, y'all! What was that? What was that?!"

The flashlight flickered and died, plunging us into black. Brian hit it against his palm, but it wouldn't do a thing. There was nothing but sky and stars and trees and us, standing out in the middle of nowhere like a human target. Another scream rent the air and faded into a low moaning.

"Do you see the headlights from here?" Brian asked.

"No," I said. Without them it was hard to tell where we'd come in. We couldn't get our bearings.

"Do you see that?" Jimmy asked. I thought maybe he was kidding around again, but then I saw it, too. A glow flared up on the horizon, near the edge of the trees across the clearing. "What the hell is that?"

The glow went out. There was a game being played, and, once again, we were losing. I counted my breaths. One, two, three, four, five . . . The clearing was alive with small fires. They popped up around the perimeter of the circle, one after another, like crazy bottle rockets, trapping us where we stood.

"Oh God, oh God!" K.J. cried.

The chanting was back and louder this time, getting closer. Something was moving out there in the mesquite trees. Hank's dream words thrummed in my ears. *There are bad things, Danny. . . .*

"Move!" Brian yelled, taking off for the trees. In the fire glow, he was just a fast-moving shadow, hard to see and impossible to follow.

"Wait up!" I yelled. But he didn't. Confused, panicked, I found myself alone, running hard as I could through unfamiliar trees. God, it was dark. Branches slapped at my hands and face. I could hear the yelps and calls of my friends, but my own frantic breathing nearly drowned them out. Finally, I didn't hear anything at all. I got turned around several times and found myself back in the clearing again. Just me, alone. And then I heard something behind me that stopped me cold.

"Danny . . . pssst, Danny . . ."

I didn't want to look. I didn't want to see him. But already my feet were starting their slow turn toward the vast dark behind me. A strange glow circled my dead brother. He didn't have a shirt on, and his skin was pale as the albino fish that live in the dark murky part of the creek behind our house.

"Danny, the bad things. They're here. You have to be careful." I tried to speak, but Hank put his finger to his blue lips. "Shhh, quiet. They'll hear you. We have to get to the graveyard."

For a second, I didn't know what to do. I followed the glow of him through the maze of trees, watching the fires burn around the clearing. The woods had gone strangely quiet. I didn't hear my friends anymore. For all I knew, they'd made it back to the car and left me out here alone. Well, not quite alone. We darted through the abandoned graves of Rosethorn, not caring that we were trampling over the dead. I was breathing hard with fear and exhaustion and something else, something I'd held back for a long time.

"Hank," I gasped out. "Hank. I need to . . . tell you something."

He stopped. "Okay."

"I'm sorry. For what I said to you that day." I started to cry then. "I'm so, so sorry."

He nodded. "Yeah, I know." He put his hand on the heavy door of a tall stone mausoleum and it opened wide. "Go on. Get in."

The tomb was pitch black and smelled like moldering leaves. Hank looked quickly toward the trees and the fires.

"Go on, Danny. It's the only way. I'll be back when it's safe."

I stepped into the dark hole, slipped, and fell. The floor was slick. When I pulled my hands away, they were covered with something I didn't even want to think about, and I quickly wiped them on my shirt. I tripped over something in the dark and it came awake in a burst of white light. A flashlight. It rolled back and forth, catching a foot in its beam. With trembling fingers, I picked it up and shone it on the spot, letting the light travel—a sneaker, jeans, Ozzy T-shirt. My whole arm started to shake, and when the light hit Brian's dead face, his eyes still open wide in terror, I started to scream. I kept screaming when I saw K.J. and Jimmy and Marla, all as dead as Brian, the blood splashed across them like paint.

Hank sidled up behind me. "Yeah," he sighed. "They were a little freaked-out to see me at first. But then I told them I'd come back to help you, that you were hurt in here, and they came just like that."

In my head, I heard myself talk, but I don't know if I did or not. Fear had thinned my mind to something brittle and close to snapping.

"I scared you guys good with the chanting and the fires, didn't I?" He smiled at me. Smiled just like the little brother I used to know, who used to ask me for soda money and give me froggers in the arm, who used to pester me with a hundred and one stupid questions. It was the kind of smile that would break your heart, if your heart wasn't a dead thing buried in the vault of your chest.

My leg felt warm and wet, and some part of me realized I'd pissed myself.

"Hey, Danny? Who do you think would win in a fair fight? Me? Or you?"

My voice came out dry and choked. "I don't want to fight you, Hank."

He pouted. "C'mon! Answer the question. For real."

In the glow of him, I saw Marla's blood-spattered hand, the hand that had been in mine.

"Y-you." I laughed sharp and hard, a laugh wavering on the edge of complete hysteria.

He grinned wide. "You know it!" He laughed, too, like it was the funniest joke he'd ever heard. "Yeah. In a fair fight. For sure."

"For sure," I echoed, my voice nothing more than a squeak now.

Hank's laugh slowed and stopped altogether. Something hard flitted across his black eyes and settled there.

"But Danny, you should know by now, there's no such thing as a fair fight."

Hank started that horrible smiling. The sharp points of his teeth gleamed white and brittle as bone. Black sludge ran from his mouth, fast and slick. "I told you the bad things were here, Danny. I just didn't tell you where."

How do you fight the devil? What do you offer to the bad things to keep them away?

A blade appeared in his hand. It glinted in the gloom. "I told you I'd scare you someday, Danny. . . ."

This is not happening. Not happening. Not. Happening.

"All you have to do is take out their hearts, Danny. . . ."

Don't scream. It's just a night terror. Like the funeral.

I could smell Hank's cold, foul breath. "Then we can be together forever. . . ."

Gotta wake up now.

"I've already done the hard part. . . ."

Wake up.

His voice boomed in the tight space. "You owe me, Danny! If you don't do it, I swear you'll be sorry!"

Wake up, wake up, oh Jesus, wake up.

"Kill or be killed, Danny. Kill or be killed. Kill or be killed. Kill—"

I screamed and the knife was everywhere. It was everywhere and my eyes were black as Hank's and I was

laughing and that made me scream even louder. I
screamed until there was no scream left in me and I was
so tired I had to close my eyes. And when I opened them
again, I found myself back out in the clearing, shivering
in the cold, totally alone. No fires. No Hank. No devil
worshippers. There was only the sky with its handful of
stars twinkling down at me.

I didn't waste any time. I stumbled through the
woods, picking up my pace till I was running hard. I
kept running, too, until I could see the bright lights of
the road. I waved down the first thing I saw. It was a big
truck, some guy heading back to the highway after a gas
up and coffee chug at the truck stop a mile to the east.
He pulled over in a hiss of brakes.

"Hey. Hey, kid. What are you doing out here? You
lost?"

I nodded.

"You okay?"

"I'm okay." My voice sounded strange to me.

"You by yourself?"

I nodded again.

He shook his head. "All right. Well, guess you better hop in, then."

I climbed up into the seat and he offered me a Coke.
I drank it down greedily. It was hot in there, so hot. . . . I
unzipped my jacket. The driver stared at my shirt.

"Jesus! You look all beaten up."

I looked down. The front of my shirt was matted with something. *What was it? Oh, right. Dried blood.* I closed my eyes and saw the blood everywhere, my hands covered in it.

"Yeah, my friends and I were pretty drunk. There was a fight. They left me there." I heard a soft, familiar laugh rumble through me. *Shut up,* I told it.

The driver grinned. "Boys will be boys, eh? And that's how you ended up lost?"

"Lost . . ." I repeated. Me, lost in the woods. Hank, taking me in. My friends on the floor. Hank, giving me the knife and guiding my hand. *"All you have to do is take out their hearts. Do it, Danny, and we can be together forever. I'll show you. It's really easy once you start. . . ."* And he was right. It was strangely easy. By the time I got to Marla I could do it with my eyes closed. I didn't feel afraid anymore. I didn't feel anything. Kill or be killed.

"I got all turned around in the dark and had to find my way out again," I answered.

Good one, Hank whispered inside my head. He giggled a little more.

"You sound like a girl," I muttered. That made Hank mad—I could tell.

"Excuse me?" The truck driver demanded.

"Nothing. Sorry. I think I bumped my head out there."

The truck driver turned his eyes back to the road. He didn't seem pissed anymore. That was a close one. I'd have to be more careful.

"So, what's your name?" he asked.

Go on. Tell him, Hank whispered in my ear. *Tell him your name.*

My name, my name. I am your fear. I am the evil that lives out there in the dark, the evil that lines the inside of men's hearts. Oh, I am the bad things, the bad things, the bad things. . . .

"Danny Turner," I said, smiling wide the way Hank would. In the side mirror, the streetlights washed over my pale face, light-dark, light-dark, my eyes going black as blood on velvet.

The driver angled the truck toward the on-ramp and into the slow bleed of car lights running along the highway in the deep, patient night.

"Well, Danny Turner, where you headed?"

I fingered the sharp blade peeking out of my jacket sleeve, an edge waiting for blood. It made me sigh. "Anywhere. Anywhere is good."

Yes, anywhere. Anywhere people stand on the hushed curve of their leafy streets, calling their kids in at dusk when the wind picks up, watching the sky for signs of a storm. Anywhere they feel the quickening of their pulses under the smooth calm of their skin at the first spat of rain, as they push their children ahead of them toward the doors, racing for the safety of their homes as the skies break open with a roar. Anywhere they peek out from windows at the crackles of vicious light striking the defenseless earth, laughing, giddy with the close call, thinking they are safe, pretending they're not waiting—breathlessly, quietly, hopefully— for the bad things to come.

The Gray Boy's Work

M. T. Anderson

When the man returned from the war, he came the last part of the voyage in a farmer's oxcart, half asleep. He brought with him an angel or a goddess seated captive beside him.

His children spied him from afar and they ran to the cart crying, "Father! It's Father!" and "Pa!" The man was shivering in the February weather and was barely able to lift his hand. The angel beside him was an Angel of Victory, and she had on her head a lantern with a candle sputtering within it. She was blindfolded.

The man's wife ran out of the house laughing with joy, and she went to his side. Even before he was lowered to the ground, she was embracing him. Their voices were small in the wide, cold fields beneath the mountains. The clouds that day were yellow and thick. The wind blew hard past the family, now reunited, and past their house and barn.

The man's eldest son, Ezra, was shy of his father, and he stood back while the other two children jumped and called their greetings. Ezra felt great relief, for his father was home and God had touched the valley with His forefinger; and the boy smiled to see his brother and sister hopping in pride and affection.

The father, set down on the ground, could not stand, and looked to Ezra for aid. Ezra's mother paid the farmer who had brought the father home on the cart.

Ezra went and stood beside his father. It felt good to offer his father an arm, a shoulder. Ezra had not seen his father for nearly two years. The father took the boy's arm and said, "You are a good boy." The mother on one side and the son on the other, they walked the father to his house. The angel followed behind, dragging her vestments through the brown snow.

The mother said to the father, "You won some great victory." She smiled and pressed his hand to her mouth.

The father did not answer.

"We saw the signs in the sky," the woman explained. "On Christmas Eve there was chariots come out of the mountains."

Jesse, the youngest son, hopped and exclaimed that there had been angels in the air playing upon Instruments of Music.

"I told the children, the trombones celestial mean just one thing," said the mother. "Triumph in New Jersey."

There was a space of white silence then, for the father looked at his children with his mouth open wide. "We won," he agreed at last. They saw that his eyes were wet.

He said, "I did not think to ever see you again in this life."

And the man held his children to him one by one, and the two young ones pranced about him. He asked to sleep, and they took him to his bed and laid him down; and they were quiet as they could be, considering their excitement at his return.

He slept heavily, with Victory seated beside him, her blindfolded face cast down.

Despair had been in the house for some months because the family had not known whether their father was alive or dead. Each day, they said their prayers for his safe return, dawn, noon, and night. But with so many months passing, and no word, they had come to a silence about it all, and finally, their prayers themselves were silent. There was work to be done, the mother said, and another day to be got through. The mother and sister baked without a word in the early morning, and the two boys scattered out to the barn, where they milked and gathered eggs; the first sunlight fell across the red mountains, and Despair sat at the table with her frown and her fangs and her hair in her eyes and watched them all.

Now, while the man slept his first sleep in his own house, Despair rose from her seat and greeted Victory. They sat together and took each other's hands. Their breath mingled by the kitchen table.

They seemed to be acquainted.

The mother watched with careful eyes the angels' soft civility.

The father slept long. Through the night, little Esther slept curled against him. She was so young she could barely remember him from when he had left for the war.

Ezra was glad for his father's sleep, because it gave him time to get all things in order for his father. Ezra wanted the barn and all of the things which had been in his care for near two years to be perfect. So while the man slept through the morning, Ezra groomed the horse and hung the tools and got the Bits, as he called his sister and his brother, to help him sweep.

Ezra saw the Apples' boy Lem walking by the stream that morning and said to him, "My father is back." Lem Apple's father had not gone to fight for the cause of the country in the war. Lem Apple stared at Ezra.

Ezra said, "He's back," and shrugged like it was nothing. "Guess he's a hero. Fought with General Washington. They won at New Jersey."

Lem Apple gaped, nodded, and kept on walking.

* * *

Victory knelt before the mother. The mother reached into the angel's lantern and pried free the candle.

She took it to the hearth, trimmed the wick, and lit it once more in the fire.

"That's better, ain't it?" she said, twisting the candle back into its socket. "Now there's a flame in your head again."

Victory smiled.

When the man awakened, he turned and saw that they had prepared the noon meal for him. He rolled off the bed and walked to the table. The woman put soup in front of him. Ezra stood across the room and watched him.

The father ate noisily and said nothing. The children did not eat. They studied their father carefully. Esther, the little girl, and Jesse, the youngest boy, sat, but they did not bother with their food. Ezra folded his hands in front of him.

They waited as long as they could, and then Jesse said, "Father, you kill any Englishmen?"

The father ate his soup and said, "We all killed some."

The mother gave another bowl to Despair. Despair was left-handed with her spoon.

"You want to see the barn?" Ezra asked. "I took real good care of it."

"I reckon you did," said the father. "You're a little man."

Ezra did not reply.

The father looked at his son. He said, "I know. You ain't little."

Ezra turned his eyes down and ate his soup.

The man had left for the war when the first call was on the land, when the redcoats had taken Boston and the people rose from all of the farms, the hills, and the villages to chase them out. One day, omens had walked across the family's fields, hand in hand, singing like glass about Necessity.

"What are they?" Ezra asked.

"They're omens," said his father.

Ezra said, "They're in the beans."

His father nodded and knocked at the dirt with his spade; he put his hand up to his brow so he could squint at the singing. Then he went across the field to talk to them. Ezra watched his father greet them and nod. And later that night, when the omens had passed over all the town, all the villagers and farmers had come together on the Green. They had gone shouting to the doctor's house, because word said that the doctor was a Tory and a redcoat-lover, and was for the king. The farmers yelled for him until he came to his front door. Then they took him and dragged him through dung, and they fed him dirt while his stuck-up daughters cried. The doctor tried to fight his neighbors with one arm, but he was not a strong man and there were forty or fifty men against him. Then the villagers threw him to the ground before the meetinghouse, and someone said, "You get out of the village before nightfall tomorrow or it won't go easy with you."

No one had seen him since.

Two days after that, Ezra's father had left to join the Patriots outside of Boston. The family heard from him when he was there and then in New York. He couldn't write, himself. The family got letters he'd had friends write for him when he reenlisted. After that, there was the silence, and months turned into a year, and no word came to the family; and Despair had arrived, eating their stew, coughing through the night, sucking softly at the white parts of their arms.

The mountains were big and pewter in the afternoon. Ezra said to his father, "You want I should show you the barn?"

The father replied, "Your mother and I got to have a walk first."

"Where you got to walk?" asked Esther.

"I got to walk with your mother," the father repeated. He gave his wife a look. They went out together. They left the children by the fireplace.

Ezra went outside to get more wood. He brought in several armloads and stacked them. He put another log on the fire so when they got back, it would still be going high. He took good care of the family. They would notice when they returned. They would comment on how, when his father was gone, Ezra watched out for the rest of them.

His little brother Jesse sat at the table and stared. He hadn't spoken or moved for some time. Ezra was tired of people just watching other people, so he said, "What ails?"

Jesse shook his head.

Ezra said, "What's the trouble?"

In a voice that was sure and that was hard as rocks, Jesse said, "Father run away. He run away from the camp before General Washington ever led that New Jersey battle."

In his stomach, Ezra felt something like a fear of dropping. He lay down the poker by the fire. He knew that it was true.

"No," he said.

Jesse held up his hands.

Ezra asked, "How do you know that?"

"I just know. That's what they're talking about. I know." He sighed. "He run away."

Despair started laughing. Jesse and Ezra turned to her. She smiled at them both.

When the man and the woman came back from their walk, the woman frowned and the man had no look at all on his face. They held each other's hands. Their children stood in the mud of the dooryard and watched them come up from the river.

The parents walked up and stood among their children.

"Now I'll look at that barn," said Ezra's father.

Ezra did not stir.

"Ezra," said the father, "let's look at that barn."

Ezra did not move. "You run away," he said to his father. "You didn't fight the battle."

"I fought battles."

"How many redcoats you kill?"

"I don't know."

"How can you not know?"

"I don't."

"How? If you killed them, how can't you know?"

"Breed's Hill," growled the father. "Battles. Boston Neck. Dorchester Heights. Long Island. Kip's Bay."

"If you killed redcoats, how's it you can't know how many?"

The father reached out and grabbed the boy's collar and dragged the boy toward him. The father's teeth were clenched. He said, "I can't know"—giving the boy a solid shake—"I can't know because when you fight in a battle, you're in lines, with lead and grapeshot filling the whole air, and everything is on fire, and your musket don't aim at nothing, and the redcoats come on at you, rank after rank, and you may see some of them fall down through the smoke, screaming, but there's a man you love's brains on your arm and his face is down by your feet, so you don't take so careful notice of which phantom got hit by which deadly part of the air." The father shook his son again.

"In battle," he said, "you load and you fire into the smoke, and you pray that the battle is already over."

He let his son go.

Ezra stumbled back. The boy straightened his smock. He looked his father in the eye.

And Ezra said, "You're a deserter."

"I fought for two years. Near enough."

"You run away. General Washington fought that battle without you."

"If you knew what that camp was like . . . the winter camp . . . If you saw that . . ."

Ezra's voice choked. "I told the Apple boy Lem that you was a hero."

"Ezra!" said the mother.

The boy was thrilled that his father looked scared now. The boy said, "I told Lem Apple that you was a hero. I guess I told him lies."

"Ezra," said the mother, "you get inside the barn. Father, you come—"

"I don't need orders from a woman," said the man; but he went inside the house all the same.

Ezra went to the barn to do chores. He was glad not having to look at his father. He was glad of being alone.

The father lay on his bed, talking to his littlest daughter. "Esther," he said, "you're my Esther. When I left home, your feet, they made tiny mouse footprints. I always said,

'Where did that mouse get into the house? Where's that little mouse?'"

She looked at her father with large and oval eyes.

He took some of her hair in his hand. "Did your brother tell you about the time he rolled you down the roof?"

There was a knock on the door. The woman answered it. It was the neighbors, the Apples, come with a friend of theirs from the next village over. They wanted to speak to the father. They were full of joy. They held their hats against their stomachs and did not know whether to sit or stand.

"Sir," said one, "we hear you fought next to General George Washington."

The father smiled faintly.

Some minutes later, Ezra came in from the barn to find them all sitting around the table. Despair hung in one corner of the house, smeared in webbing. Her eyes blinked white. Victory stood facing the fire.

". . . So we chased them across the river," the father was saying. "And we threw into it all their furniture, all their tents . . ."

Ezra stood with his arms crossed.

His father said, "Later, they burned most of New York. I don't rightly know who burned it. They did. We did. Someone burned it."

Ezra watched his father. The father's eyes did not meet his son's.

"Mr. Brainerd," said the Apple husband, pointing at his friend from the next village, "Mr. Brainerd here fought down in New York. You know each other?"

The father rubbed his mouth with his hand and kept rubbing.

"It's a pleasure to meet you, sir," said Mr. Brainerd.

"It is a pleasure," said the father.

"I reckon I seen you about the camp."

The father nodded, with his hand still on his mouth.

"That was truly a time," said Mr. Brainerd. "That was a time. Your tales do bring it back. I wish I could've fought alongside you at New Jersey. I was sent away for my leg."

The father agreed carefully, "It was truly a time."

The son still watched, his face clean of emotion.

"I missed the tales," said the son.

"I can tell you another time," said his father.

The son glared. The father could not abide his son's look and stood up to fix something, anything. "We got any . . . we got any cake," he asked his wife, "we could give them a piece of?"

"Well," said the wife, "I believe we got—"

"He run away," announced Ezra.

Everyone looked at Ezra.

"He run away. From the camp."

The father made a move to throw a cup. He set it down instead and turned away to touch the wall.

The guests watched him.

The father turned halfway toward them, as if to speak, then faced the wall again. He lay both of his hands on the plaster.

The Apples looked at each other. Mr. Brainerd smacked his lips.

Ezra went to the fire and made like he was propping it up.

The wife went to stand by her husband. She put her arm around him.

"I reckon," said one of the Apples, "that we've stayed long enough."

They rose to leave.

As they opened the door, the father turned toward them. He said, "We ate candles. We boiled our own shoes to make a broth. Mr. Brainerd, you tell them."

"You're lucky to be alive, sir," said Mr. Brainerd. "Lucky you're not hanged. I got to get back over the mountain."

"We boiled shoes. I et leather."

Mr. Apple said, "This is your own . . . your . . ." He waved his hand.

"There was smallpox," said the father. "Men dying. Most of the men. Tell them. I prayed for mercy. I never had the smallpox. A man in my tent, he had it. They wouldn't move me."

"Sir," said Mr. Apple, "we have a great many chores."

"The snow was high and we didn't have no shoes after a time. We was drilling barefoot in the snow. Men were dying. Boys were covered in sores. There wasn't any food."

His wife said, "He is still a hero."

"I fought two years for this country," said the father. "Congress called, and I went."

"That's right," said Mr. Apple, rattling the latch. "Good-day, then."

Ezra watched this all unfold. He watched the Apples and their friend leave. The mother sat.

The father still spoke, but now to the closed door, where the winter was.

"I seen men's arms," said the father. "I seen men's arms in a stack where they been sawed." He put his hands over his eyes. "And I thought to myself, 'I want to be able to hold my children when I get home.'"

Ezra, lying on his mattress in the loft, could hear his parents talk. He listened to hear if there would be anything that might change something somehow.

At one time, his mother said, "Ezra brought in more wood," and the father made a noise that meant, "So he did." They busied themselves making a fire to keep the cottage warm through the night.

At another time the father said, "That fence up to the Mastersons' got to be repaired."

And at another time, the mother said, "We smoked our own pig this year," and the father said, "Had a fine flavor at supper."

There was no word of desertion.

Still, Ezra lay waiting for some argument that would free his father of the charge.

The next morning, Despair wore the blindfold, and Victory had the fangs. Ezra found them sitting in the barn when he went out to tend to the animals.

The boy stood in the darkness of dawn and looked at Victory. The door of the broken lantern upon her head creaked closed as she turned to look back at him. Her eyes were not the eyes of a person, but were golden.

"Miss," he said, "you took off the blindfold."

She shook her head slowly.

He did not like talking to someone with fangs.

"I got to feed all the animals," he said. "Could you go outside?"

The angels rose to their feet. Their garments were dusted with straw from where they had slept. Ezra stepped backward. They were as tall as he was. The barn was dark and cold. He backed against the wall. He watched the golden eyes and they watched him.

For a time, they did not move. He said, "Pardon me, Miss Victory. Miss Despair."

"You mistook," whispered Victory. "She ain't Despair. She's Prayer."

Victory and Prayer turned. Prayer stumbled toward the door, blinded, legs straight, feeling her way with her paws.

The door closed behind them.

Ezra made sure that they were gone before he knelt by the cows.

That morning, the plains between the mountains were purple with the cold.

The boy and his father walked along the edge of a field. The boy said, "I know the paddock fence up near the Mastersons' wants mending."

The father nodded.

"I was set to do it," said the boy. "I would've done it this week."

They walked on for a ways. Their old hide shoes crackled on the frozen dirt.

Suddenly, the boy said, "I'm set to do it today."

"What?"

"Mend the paddock fence."

The father nodded, but said, "Can't today. Too cold to work with wood."

"I'll do it," said the boy. "This instant." He turned away from his father and started walking quickly back to the house and the barn for tools.

"Ezra," said the father, "you can't today. It's all frozen. The wood. The sap. You can't."

The boy walked faster. The father watched him go.

Some minutes later, Ezra passed his father. He was headed for a small stand of trees. He carried an ax.

Ezra went among the trees. Their bark was gray or black. The breeze was frigid in the copse.

The boy could feel the father enter the copse behind him. The boy did not turn to face his father. He tugged on branches. He reflected that he was engaged in his own work, come what might.

He found a limb that he thought would be fine for the paddock fence. His father could not complain of it. It was a fine limb.

The boy began to strike at it with his ax. The father stood off some ways and watched.

The wood was resilient with the cold. The ax bounced back. The boy struck harder. It made no difference. The ax did nothing.

"Ezra," said the father, saying his son's name softly. "You don't have to show me."

The boy kept smacking the tree limb. The ax did nothing but chip the bark and then spring away.

"Ezra."

The boy looked up, and saw that Victory and Prayer walked across the field.

He lowered the ax.

Behind them was a boy of Ezra's age.

The procession—two angels, one boy—reached the copse. The father did not look at the three who approached. He waited, as if for a catastrophe; he studied a place where a tree had been torn out of the ground; his whole face scowled with anger and concern.

His son walked to his side. Father and son stood together.

Victory and Prayer parted. The boy behind them
limped forward. He was gray and did not have the flesh
of the living. He could not walk straight, as something
had happened to his leg.

"Get away with you," said the father. "We don't want
you here."

"Who is he?" asked the son.

"I'm a hired hand," said the gray boy in a gentle, rasp-
ing voice. "I do work of all kinds."

"Where are you from?" asked the son. "I don't know
you."

The gray boy gestured to the father. "He knows me,"
said the gray boy. "I come from under the mountain."

Victory smiled.

"Get away with you," said the father.

"I am here to help," said the gray boy. "These excellent spirits will convey me to your house, where I shall
receive my first meal. Once I have eaten of your food,
then I am bound to work."

"We don't wish you to stay," said the father, but the
angels and the boy had turned already and were walking
out of the copse.

They walked across the field. The father and son
stood by the stone wall and watched the gray boy limp
toward their home.

When the father and the son returned to the house in a
few hours, the gray boy was carrying stones. Victory

walked behind the gray boy, her hands folded near her stomach. She smiled as he staggered lamely beneath the weight of the stones.

"I'll set it down here," said the gray boy.

He fell to his knees and dropped the stone on the ground near a wall made of rocks. He had built the wall with impossible speed.

The father could not even bring himself to look at the gray boy. He pinched at his eyes with his fingers and walked into the house.

His wife was directing the making of butter. "Sprinkle in the salt," she said to little Esther. "Just so. And lay the carrot across it." When she saw her son and husband come in, she announced, "There's another one of them come. A gray boy."

The father said nothing.

Ezra said, "We already seen him."

"He says he'll aid 'round the house," the mother noted. "That's welcome."

Jesse and Ezra watched each other's faces. Jesse went outside.

The mother said, "He already split shingles for the barn roof and builded some fashion of wall. He's quick. I don't think he's of this world."

Ezra followed his brother.

When the two of them were alone in the barn, with the animals shifting all around them in the darkness, Jesse whispered, "I know who he is."

"Who?" asked Ezra.

"The gray boy."

"I meant, who is he?"

"He's a boy got killed in Father's regiment. Come for something."

Ezra fit his thumbnail into a crack in the wall. He worked his thumb up and down the crack.

"We don't need Father here," said Ezra. "It's ours now." He pointed at a trough. "I built that." He pointed at the hay. "We brought that hay in. It was about to rain for a week, and we got it all in on time."

Jesse perched on a rail. He drew his knees up to his chin. He teetered there and listened to his brother.

Ezra said, "The fields gave it all to us. I stood there every day and prayed to the hills."

Jesse nodded, breathing through his mouth. Finally, he said, "What'd you ask for?"

"That I'd get through a day," said Ezra. "That there wouldn't be no fire or drought." Ezra knocked absently on the wall. He finished, "I prayed that he would come home."

Later in the afternoon, when the father and the son were working in the yard, they saw neighbors walk slowly by. The neighbors were there to gawk at the deserter, the man who had abandoned General Washington's camp.

The father and the son lifted stones onto the wall and nestled them so the stones wouldn't rock uneasily.

The minister went by. He did not greet the father. He did not even look directly at the father. He greeted the son—"Good day, sir! You are well, I hope! Woodpile looks most impressive!"—as one would greet a man who owned a broad farm and who worked it diligently every day.

"Thank you, sir," said the son.

The father lowered his head. He kept on picking up stones.

The minister walked on.

The son, suddenly, laughed at his stooping father's back. It was a harsh, short laugh.

The father threw down his stone and walked away.

The son felt a sickness in his arms, a weakness, as if he had just been rebuked.

The father stalked across the dooryard toward the barn. His lips were slewed to one side. His shoes scraped on the frozen ground.

The gray boy stumbled around the corner of the barn. He held the pieces of the ax in his hands.

"I tried to mend the fence," he said to the father. "I tried to cut some branches." He started crying. "It broke. The ax broke into splinters." The head had come off the haft.

The father took the pieces from the gray boy. "Go inside," he said.

"Back at home I had a little ax for play."

"I reckon you did."

The gray boy wiped his eyes with his dirty wrists. He stared at the father. He turned and went inside.

When Ezra went into the house a few minutes later, wringing out his hands to warm them, he found the gray boy sitting by the fire on a stool, drinking cream out of a bowl.

"What's he doing there?" said Ezra.

"Leave him be," said Ezra's mother. "He's upset."

The gray boy looked at Ezra like he planned to kill him.

Glaring at Ezra, hunched over his bowl, the gray boy lapped the cream. His tongue was gray, too, and a full foot long.

Later that night, Ezra's mother asked the gray boy to fetch some squash up out of the cellar. The gray boy said politely that it would be most agreeable to do so. He stepped across Prayer's tail and swung open the trapdoor in the floor.

They all, shuffling around the cottage, had to step across Prayer's tail.

When the gray boy returned, he had two squash in his hands. The mother went to cut the first of them, then threw down the knife in anger.

The squash had rotted. Its insides were black, dry, and fibrous.

The second the boy had brought up was the same. She went down to find another and discovered that the lot of them had rotted.

Ezra witnessed all of this.

He watched from the table. He watched the gray boy apologize: "Ma'am, I must have jinxed the squash. It was me, surely." Ezra saw his mother tell the gray boy not to be ridiculous, that a body doesn't jinx squash. The gray boy apologized again, sneaking looks at Ezra.

The girl Esther told the gray boy to stop apologizing and go out into the yard with her. They went outside, the gray boy's lame leg clattering against the doorframe.

Ezra and his father watched each other.

"I know what you believe," said Ezra's father. "You believe he's a dead boy from my regiment. You reckon he's come to haunt me."

Ezra looked his father in the eye.

"That ain't what he is," said Ezra's father. "He's something much worse, because he won't ever go away. He'll be with you always."

"I don't want to sleep near him. He gave me a look."

"Both of you need to stop that," said the mother.

The father said, "I don't know what I've done to us all. But I did it because I . . ." He would not say anything further. He rose and put on his coat and his hat. He went outside.

Ezra lay his head down on the table but did not close his eyes.

In the late afternoon, snow began to fall over the valley. Ezra stood near the pigs and looked up at the sky. The snow had not been announced by wind. The pigs were not comfortable with the snow. They stood near the door and dipped their heads as if expecting the blow of the ax.

Ezra shooed the pigs toward their pen. He was worried that it would be too cold in the barn. He thought he should maybe get the Bits and lead some of the animals into the house.

Jesse walked into the barn, a scarf around most of his face. He walked over to Ezra.

"The gray boy ruined the beans," he said. "Mother asked him to cut some beans from the cellar and they're all over with webs and blight."

Ezra frowned and nodded.

Together, they walked to the house.

Inside, the gray boy was crying before an audience. Ezra's mother petted the gray boy's head. Little Esther and the father watched from the other side of the table.

"I'm too hurt to do anything," said the gray boy. "It's my leg. It ruins everything for you."

"Now, that's nonsense," Ezra's mother said. "Your leg don't ruin anything."

Ezra took a seat next to his father. His father inclined his head to welcome Ezra. Ezra saw his father's mouth.

They watched the gray boy nestle his head up against Ezra's mother's bosom. The gray boy wiped his eyes and stared at Ezra and the father. The gray boy's face was stark and unsmiling. Neither was it wet with tears. For the mother's sake, the gray boy made a fake sound like sobs.

Ezra and his father both put their hands on their laps. They looked at one another, united for a moment in their hatred of the crippled child's tyranny.

Ezra's father reached out and put his hand on Ezra's shoulder.

At his father's touch, Ezra remembered that he was supposed to hate his father. He sat with his father's hand weighing on his shoulder like an unuseful ornament. He could not, for a moment, remember his fury with his father. The hand lay there; Ezra tried to recall why it should not.

While he waited to remember his anger, he picked up the hand like a clod of dirt and dumped it from him.

The father was startled.

Ezra watched his father get angry. He started to cower; he could tell that his father's anger would be great.

Victory came climbing out of the loft, with a rope tied to Prayer's arm. Victory looked down upon them all from the loft, her body raked to the side by the tug of the rope.

The father rose from his seat. Ezra pushed his own chair backward. He put his palm on the edge of the table, ready to stand.

"I am tired," said the father to Ezra, "of your looks. I'm tired of your airs. I only been back two days, and I'm

tired of you not saying—" He could not continue. He
rapped once on the table like a spirit.

Ezra rose warily. He watched as his father tried to
collect words and failed.

Failing, the father paced across the room, edging
around the mother and the gray boy, and seized a red
plate from the cabinet.

He hurled it at Ezra. It broke against the table and
splinters of it hit the chair.

Ezra saw that his father was a little man. He saw
that his father was a little man who danced across the
room to get a piece of crockery to smash. He was a little
man who had to stage and act out his own fit like a
schoolgirl.

Ezra's mother had her arms around the gray boy, her
mouth open. Esther was starting to cry; Jesse had turned
away and was looking at something else.

Ezra did not think anything was funny, but he
smiled anyway, thinking of his father as a schoolgirl
who had run away and now pranced around the room
looking for crockery to smash. "I hate you," he said.

His father's shoulders were low. "Of course you
do," he said.

"I'm going to take care of the sheep."

"You should," said the father.

Esther said Ezra's name and held out her hand.

Ezra left the house.

Up on the hillside, the snow churned in great tides, driven by the darkness of night. Ezra made his way along the path.

Jesse came running behind him. "I'll help," said Jesse.

"There ain't no need to," said Ezra.

"You can't drive sheep alone," said Jesse.

They walked in silence. Sometimes the wind rose and they held on to their hats.

They reached a hut made of rough piled stones on the hilltop. The door was closed, and three sheep were milling uneasily inside. Ezra let them amble by him. He and Jesse clucked to them and started to drive them down the hill.

"He didn't mean it," said Jesse.

They had made it only a hundred yards or so when one of the sheep spooked at something by the wall and ran off to the side. The other two sheep did not notice, blinded as they were by the snow.

Jesse ran after the one. He called her name and scampered away over stones and hummocks.

The mountains were no longer clear. The only forms were the folds of the air limned by the snow.

Ezra kept on down the hillside after the other two, who blinked at the great flakes that fell on their eyelashes.

The two sheep came to the gate and stile. Ezra had left the gate open. The sheep ran through the gate, past the figure of a boy.

Ezra stopped.

It was not Jesse.

The gray boy stood on the path, his lamed foot crooked on the ground.

Ezra went to stalk past the boy.

"I am from under the mountain," said the gray boy.

"Could you kindly step—"

"I've sailed on rivers of ice."

The boy reached out and threw Ezra to the ground.

Ezra's arm was hurt on the stone wall; his back was hurt on the frozen dirt. He lay and tried to get up. Sore, he rose.

The gray boy had not moved.

Ezra leaped past the gray boy, but the gray boy's hands seized him and tossed him to the side. Ezra's ribs hit the gate, and he stumbled. This time he did not fall. The gray boy was strong and did not move.

"Get out of the way," said Ezra. "The sheep are running."

The gray boy's mouth opened, and his tongue snaked out slowly. The snow blew between them.

Ezra turned and ran back up the hill, calling Jesse's name. He did not know what was happening.

The gray boy kept pace with him.

Ezra was amazed. Even with the limp, the gray boy ran at his speed.

The gray boy took Ezra's arms and began to steer him.

"Jesse!" hollered Ezra.

He fell to his knees so he would not be led. The gray boy stopped and dragged him across the ground. Ezra struggled, but the gray boy had him; Ezra's face scraped over frost and stone.

They were headed for the hut. Snow slanted across Ezra's eyes. He did not have a lantern, and it was almost dark.

They reached the hut. Ezra jammed his leg against the stone wall. The gray boy threw Ezra into the darkness.

Ezra yelled for help. He called for Jesse and Esther and for his father.

The gray boy said, "Your father asked me to do this. He wishes you to learn. You hurt him." He slammed the wooden door, and the latch fell into place. "I am the boy he always wanted. I am not afraid."

"Let me be," demanded Ezra.

"Prayer brought me," said the boy. "And Victory."

Ezra was alone in the shed. The wind blew between the stones.

He called his brother's name. The gale from the mountains was huge, however, much vaster than his breath. He could feel the weight of the falling snow.

He heard the scrape of the gray boy's limp, circling the hut.

He backed against the wall next to the door. If the gray boy came in, he would offer an ambush. But now he could not hear any movement outside, other than the wind.

He stood alone in the hut. The snow fell over the mountains.

He wished to relax his arms, but he could not, because the cold was so heavy all around him. The air felt thick like water.

After a time, he squatted. He drew his knees up to his chest, hoping in that way to keep some of his heat clutched to him.

He did not know when his family would come for him. He did not know if they would come at all. The gray boy may have spoken the truth: his father might be sitting grimly in the house, waiting for a lesson to be learned out in the sheep shed.

Ezra beat on the old door. The door was so unfair, he could not conceive of it as solid. He rammed his shoulder against it. It did not yield.

Snow, he knew, was now piling on the other side of the door. He battered the planks and screamed. Nothing stirred. No one came.

After a while, he sat again. His senses were of no use to him.

He did not trust the darkness. Anything could be in the darkness. He imagined the arms that his father had seen stacked; he imagined revenants that sought their arms. They could be looking with eyes of accusation at the son of the traitor. They hung trailing around him. He thought he felt them. He did not fear ghostly retribution; but he feared the weight of their sadness, the infinite sadness that comes of an infinite blank and them dead forever.

The darkness seemed many-handed, groping.

He squatted near the door. He pressed his fingers between his thighs to keep them warm. He wrapped them together as fists.

Later, he breathed upon them.

He felt that time had smeared. He could no longer reckon by hours.

He remained in one place. He altered his squat. He hunkered.

He had seen men with frostbite. There was a man who lived in the next village whose face was a mask and whose hands were lopped stumps, pollarded like trees, cut back to the branch.

Ezra shook out his hands, hoping to unsettle the ice in them. He could not feel much. His breath itself was getting cold.

He sat immobile.

He imagined the gray boy standing with his father on the field of battle. He imagined his father and mother taking in the gray boy as their own son. He imagined himself dead, wandering through the frozen pastures with snow blown through his face and his chest and his legs, and he watched the new family labor in the barn, which did not seem to be his. He pictured the gray boy in his place growing old.

After some time, the world no longer rendered meaning to him. He thought about the house and the fireplace in the house, but there no longer seemed to be a difference between one thing and another thing. He could not tell the difference between the house and the hearth and the fire. They seemed to be of one substance. He knew that there was a difference between touching the stone of the fireplace and touching the fire itself, but it seemed to him, everything burned to the touch. The ground beneath him burned. The walls burned.

The sky burned, as it was said it would burn in the hour of Last Things.

The snow came down out of the sky upon him. He could see nothing.

He heard his father call, "I will search the shed!"

Ezra made a noise that he thought would identify him.

He heard his father call his name. His father was by the door.

There was a voice from down the hill. It was the gray boy. "I cannot climb there on my own. Come lift me, sir."

Ezra made a noise, but it was too soft.

"Up here," said his father.

"I cannot walk there," said the gray boy. "But that was not the way he ran. He ran toward the mountains."

Ezra turned to his side and tried slapping the planks of the door. His hands were not solid. The cold had melted them.

"Come down this path," said the gray boy. "I am not mistaken. I saw him light out for the hills."

Ezra was terrified by his own silence. The father was hesitating; not opening the door. The father was going to remove himself.

Ezra swayed his body. He pictured his father in the cart; his own leaping joy at the sight of his father; the desire to touch the man again, simply to touch him, and know him real.

Ezra slammed his head into the door.

"I'll be down," said the father, "soon as I check the shed."

"He ran off to the mountain," said the gray boy, "reviling you as he ran."

Ezra battered the door with his blunt and senseless palms.

"You hear . . . ?"

"I heard he called you coward."

"So he may have," said the father.

"Follow me," said the gray boy.

"You lie," said the father outside the door, suddenly sounding certain. "I know you lie."

And Ezra, seeing the father smile in the cart, smile to be home, beat at the door with his limbs.

He no longer knew what he saw.

Light—he knew that—and the hands reaching out to take him.

There was snow all around him, white and gentle as it fell.

The mother; the father. Victory was there, and Prayer. Out of all their mouths came scrolls, unfurled commentary, but he could not read. Jesse's scroll was golden. The snow fell over the pastures, and a family was together in the night. Everyone pointed at things that meant so much to him; his own face, among them.

They hugged him. They cried. They had been searching the way to the mountains for hours.

They lifted him up and carried him.

In the sky above the valley and the mountains, an eagle flew with yellow eyes, and its talons dragged the legend and the compass rose through the storm.

In the morning, Ezra awoke to find he could not see. He reached up and touched a blindfold. He was lying next to the fire. He fumbled in the grit around him.

"Rest," said his mother. "The angels put the blindfolds on you and your father while you were asleep. They're gone."

Ezra sat up.

"Sad you didn't get the fangs instead," said Jesse. "You could've opened oysters with your mouth."

Blindfolded, Ezra and his father ate a slow breakfast together at the table. When Ezra felt his father reaching for the ewer, he reached out his own hand and took his father's wrist. His father paused, then patted his son's arm. For a long time, they remained like that.

Ezra's father asked, "Is he smiling?"

"Neither of you's smiling," said Ezra's mother. She laughed and touched the father's cheek.

"Where's the gray boy?" Ezra asked.

"Up in the sheep shed," said Jesse. "He says he won't come down. He says people don't understand how hard it is to live with a leg like his."

After breakfast, father and son went out into the dooryard together. They moved slowly, with their hands outstretched. Together, father and son felt their way across the snow. They touched rock wall and empty hayrick. They ran their fingers across the wood of the barn.

They could feel the sun on their faces.

They spent the long morning after that snowfall together, stumbling, catching each other's arms; and they thanked God for the blindfolds upon them, which hid, so they might see all anew.

The Poison Eaters

Holly Black

I trust that your bonds are not too tight, my son. Please don't struggle. Don't bother. You're soft. All princes are soft, and these cells are built for hardened men.

It is a shame that you never met your grandmother. You are very alike with your tempers and your rages. I imagine she would have doted on you. How ironic that Father tried her for being a poisoner. Right now, especially, Paul, I imagine irony is much on your mind.

The morning of her execution she had her attendants dress her all in red and braid her hair with fresh roses. Wine-colored stones cluttered her fingers. There are several paintings of it; she died opulently. It was drizzling. I was to walk her to her tomb. It was something like a wedding processional as she took my arm and we went together, down the steep steps. The place was dark and stank of incense. My mother leaned close to me and whispered that I looked splendid in black. I remember not being able to say anything, only taking her hand and pressing it. Outside, the rain began to fall hard. We heard the shrieks of the assemblage; aristocrats don't like to be wet.

My mother smiled and said, "I bet they wish they were down here."

I forced a smile and made myself kiss her cheek and bid her farewell. The masons were waiting at the top of the stairs.

My mother and I were not close, but she was still my mother. I was a dutiful son. I had commanded the cooks to put the sharpest of my hunting knives beneath the food they had prepared for her. I wonder if you would do that for me, Paul. Perhaps you would. After all, it cost me nothing to be kind.

See this cup? A beautiful thing, solid gold, one of the few treasures of our family that remain. It was my father's. He had a cupbearer bring him his wine in it, even as his other guests drank from silver. I have it here beside me, just as you filled it—half with poison and half with cider, so that it will go down easy.

I have a story to tell you. You've always been restless: too busy to hear stories of people long dead and secrets that no longer matter. But now, Paul, bound and gagged as you are, you can hardly object to my telling you a tale.

* * *

Sometimes at night the three sisters would sleep in one bed, limbs tangling together. Despite that, they would never get warm. Their lips would stay blue and sometimes one of them would shake or cramp, but they were used to that. Sometimes, in the mornings, when serving women would bring them their breakfasts, one might touch them by accident and the next day she would be missing. But they were used to that, too. Not that they did not grieve. They often wept. They wept over the mice they would find, stiff and cold, on the stone floor of their chamber; over the hunting dogs that would run to them when they were out walking on the hills, jumping up and then falling down; over the butterfly that once landed on Mirabelle's cheek for a moment, before spiraling to the ground like a bit of paper.

One winter, their father gave them lockets. Each locket had the painting of a boy inside of it. They took turns making up stories about the boys. In one story, Alice's picture, who they'd taken to calling Nicholas, was a knight with a silver arm, questing after a sword cooled from the forge in the blood of sirens. At night, the sword became a siren with hair as black as ink, and Nicholas fell in love with her. At this point the story stopped because Alice stormed off, annoyed that Cecily had made up a story where the boy from her locket fell in love with someone else.

Each day they would eat a salad of what looked like flowering parsley. Afterward, their hands would tremble and they would become so cold that they had to sit close to the fire and scorch themselves. Sometimes their father came in and watched them eat, but he was careful never to touch them. Instead, he would read them prayers or lecture on the dangers of sloth and the importance of needlework. Occasionally, he would have one of them read from Homer.

Summer was their favorite time. The sun would warm their sluggish blood and they would lie out in the garden like snakes. It was on one of those jaunts that the blacksmith's apprentice first spotted Alice. He started coming around a lot after that, reading his weepy poetry and trying to get her to pay him attention. Before long, Alice was always crying. She wanted to go to him, but she dared not.

"He's not the boy in your locket," Mirabelle said.

"Don't be stupid." Alice wiped her reddened eyes. "Do you think that we're supposed to marry them and be their wives? Do you think that's why we have those lockets?"

Cecily had been about to say something and stopped. She'd always thought the boys in the lockets would be theirs someday, but she did not want to say so now, in case Alice called her stupid, too.

"Imagine any of us married. What would happen then, sisters? We are merely knives in the process of being sharpened."

"Why would Father do that?" Cecily demanded.

"Father?" Alice demanded. "Do you really think he's your father? Or mine? Look at us. How could you, Mirabelle, be short and fair, while Cecily is tall and dark? How could I have breasts like melons, while hers are barely currants? How could we all be so close in age? We three are no more sisters than he is our father."

Mirabelle began to weep. They went to bed that night in silence, but when they awoke, Mirabelle would no longer eat. She spat out her bitter greens, even when she became tired and languid. Cecily begged her to take something, telling her that they were sisters no matter what.

"Different mothers could explain our looks," Alice said, but she did not sound convinced, and Mirabelle would not be comforted.

Their father tried to force Mirabelle to eat, but she pushed food into her cheek only to spit it out again when he was gone. She got thinner and more wan, her body shriveling, but she did not die. She faded into a thin wispy thing, as ephemeral as smoke.

"What does it mean?" Cecily asked.

"It means she shouldn't be so foolish," said their father. He tried to tempt her with a frond of bitter herb in a gloved hand, but she was so insubstantial that she passed through him without causing harm and drifted out to the gardens.

"It's my fault," said Alice.

But the ghostly shape of Mirabelle merely laughed her whispery laugh.

The next day Alice went out to meet the blacksmith's apprentice and kissed him until he died. It did not bring her sister back. It did not help her grief. She built a fire and threw herself on it. She burned until she was only a blackened shadow.

No tears were enough to express how Cecily felt, so her eyes remained dry as her sisters floated like shades through the halls of the estate and her father locked himself in his study.

As Cecily sat alone in a dim room, her sisters came to her.

"You must bury us," Alice said.

"I want it to be in the gardens of one of our suitors. Together so that we won't be lonely."

"Why should I? Why should I do anything for you?" Cecily asked. "You left me here alone."

"Stop feeling sorry for yourself," said Alice. Lack of corporeal form had not made her any less bossy.

"We need you," Mirabelle pleaded.

"Why can't you bury yourselves? Just drift down into the dirt."

"That's not the way it works," Mirabelle told her.

And so, with a sigh of resignation, gathering up the lockets of her sisters, Cecily left the estate and began to walk. She was not sure where she was headed, but the road led to town.

It was frightening to be on her own, with no one to brush her hair or tell her when to sit down to lunch. The forest sounded strange and ominous.

She stopped and paid for an apple with a silver ring. As she passed a stall, she overheard one of the merchants say, "Look at her blue mouth, her pale skin. She's the walking dead." As soon as he said it, Cecily knew it to be true. That was why Alice and Mirabelle would not die. They were already dead.

She walked for a long time, resting by a stream when she was tired. After she rose, she saw the imprint of herself in the withered grass. Tears rolled over her cheeks and dampened the cloth of her dress, but one fell where ants scurried and stilled them. After that, Cecily was careful not to cry.

At the next town, she showed the pictures in each of the lockets to the woman who sold wreaths for graves. She knew only the first boy. His name was Vance—not Nicholas—and he was the son of a wealthy landowner to the east who had once paid her for a hundred wreaths of chrysanthemums to decorate the necks of horses on Vance's twelfth birthday.

Cecily started down the winding and dusty road east. Once she was given a ride on a wagon filled with hay. She kept her hands folded in her lap, and when the farmer reached out to touch her shoulder in kindness, she shied away as though she despised him. The coldness in his eyes afterward hurt her, and she tried not to think of him.

Another traveler demanded the necklace of opals she wore at her throat, but she slapped him and he fell, as if struck by a blow more terrible than any her soft hand should have delivered.

Her sisters chattered at her as she went. Sometimes their words buzzed around her like hornets; sometimes they went sulkily silent. Once, Mirabelle and Alice had a fight about which of their deaths was more foolish and Cecily had to shout at them until they stopped.

Cecily often got hungry, but there was no salad of bitter parsley, so she ate other leaves and flowers she picked in the woods. Some of them filled her with that familiar cold shakiness while others went down her throat without doing anything but sating her. She drank from cool streams and muddy puddles, and by the time she reached Vance's estate, her shoes were riddled with holes.

The manor house was at the top of a small hill, and the path was set with smooth, pale stones. The door was a deep red, the color berries stain eager fingers. Cecily rapped on the door.

The servants saw her tattered finery and brought her to Master Hornpull. He had white hair that fell to his shoulders, but the top of his pate was bald, shining with oil, and slightly sunburned.

Cecily showed him the locket with Vance's picture and told him about Alice's death. He was kind and did not mention the state of Cecily's clothing or the strangeness of her coming so suddenly and on foot. He told servants to prepare a room for her and let her wash herself in a tub with golden faucets in the shape of swans.

"If you kiss him once, then I will be able to kiss him forever and ever," Alice told her as she dried off.

"I thought you liked the blacksmith's apprentice," Cecily said.

"I always liked Nicholas better." Alice's ghostly voice sounded snappish.

"Vance," Cecily corrected.

Servants came to ask Cecily if she would go to dinner, but she begged off, pleading weariness. She planned to doze on the down mattress until nightfall, when she could steal out to the gardens, but there was a sharp rap on the door and her father walked into the room.

Cecily made a poorly concealed gasp and struggled to stand. For a moment, she was afraid, without really knowing why.

He pushed back graying hair with a gloved hand. "How fortunate that you are so predictable. I was quite worried when I found you had gone."

"I was too sad to be there alone," Cecily said. She could not meet his eyes.

"You must marry Vance in Alice's place."

"I can't," Cecily said. What she meant was that Alice would be mad, and indeed, Alice was already darting around, muttering furiously.

"You can and you will," her father said. "Every thing yearns to do what it is made for."

Cecily said nothing. He drew from his pocket a neck-lace of tourmalines and fastened them at her throat. "Be as good a girl as you are lovely," he said. "Then we will go home."

The earliest memory Cecily had of her father was of gloved hands, mail-over-leather, checking her gums. She had been very sick for a long time, lying on mounds of hay in a stinking room full of sick little girls. She remem-bered his messy hair and his perfectly trimmed beard and the way his smile had seemed aimed in her direc-tion but not for her. "Little girls are like oysters," he told her as he pried her eyelids wide. "Just as a grain of sand irritates the oyster into making nacre, so your dis-comfort will make something marvelous."

"Who are you?" she had asked him.

"Don't you remember?" he had said. "I'm your father."

That had upset her, because she must be very sick indeed to not know her own father, but he told her that she had died and come back to life, so it was natural that she'd forgotten things. He lifted her up with his gloved hands and carried her out of the room. She re-membered seeing other sick girls on the hay, their eyes sunken and dull and their bodies very still. That, she wouldn't have minded forgetting.

Cecily thought of those girls as she drifted off to sleep in the vast and silky bed Master Hornpull provided for her, cooled by the twining limbs of her ghostly sisters.

The next day, Cecily's face was painted: her mouth made vermillion, her eyelids smeared with cerulean, her cheeks rouged rose. They had brought pots of white stuff to smear on her skin, but she was already so pale there was no need. Cecily waved the servants off and pinned up her hair herself. She wasn't very good at it and locks tumbled down over her shoulders. Mirabelle assured her that it looked better that way. Alice told her that she looked like a mess. Mirabelle said that Alice was just jealous. That might have been true; Alice had always been a jealous person.

In the parlor downstairs, Cecily's father grabbed her elbow with one gloved hand and spoke through a broad, forced smile.

Vance was nothing like their made-up stories. He was short and slender, but handsome just the same. They danced and Cecily was conscious of the warmth of his hands through the fabric of her dress and the satin of her gloves, but she was even more conscious of the tender glances he gave to a small, curvy girl in a golden gown.

"He would have liked me," Alice crowed. "I am exactly the kind of girl he likes."

"Maybe you should have thought of that before you—" Cecily started, forgetting for a moment that she was speaking to the dead. Vance turned toward her, face flaming and lips spilling apology.

But when the priest asked Cecily to take Vance in marriage, she was named as Mirabelle. She repeated the words anyway.

"Does that mean Nicholas is mine?" Mirabelle whispered, her ghostly voice filled with surprised delight. He was her clear favorite in the stories. Cecily had made the boy in Mirabelle's locket too bookish for her tastes.

"Vance," Cecily corrected under her breath.

"Kill him already," Alice hissed. "Stop mooning around."

And, indeed, Vance was leaning toward Cecily to seal their vows with a kiss. She pulled back at the last moment, so that his mouth merely brushed her veil, then tried to smile in apology. As she turned to depart the ceremony with her new husband, she saw her father in the crowd. He nodded once in her direction.

At the party following the wedding, one of the guests remarked to Cecily how good it was that her father was taking an interest in society again, after falling out of favor with the king.

"He seldom talks to me about politics," Cecily said. "I did not know he was ever a friend of his Majesty."

The woman who had said it looked around, seemingly torn between guilt and gossip. "Well, it was when the king was only the youngest prince. No one expected him to take the throne, because his father was so young and his two older brothers so healthy. But illness took all three of them, one after another, and once his Majesty was on the throne, your father was well favored. He was given money and lands beyond most of our—well, you know how vast and lovely your father's land is."

"Yes," Cecily said, feeling very stupid. She had never wondered where these things came from. She had merely assumed that there had always been plenty and there would always be plenty.

"But after the prince was born, your father fell out of favor. The king would no longer see him."

"Why?" Cecily asked.

"As if I know!" The woman laughed. "He really has kept you in another world up there!"

Later, Cecily went to a large bedchamber and changed into a pale shift that was still, somehow, darker than her skin. She stared at her arms, looking at the tracery of purple veins, mapping a geography of paths she might take, a maze of choices she did not know her way out of.

"You look cold," Vance said. "I could warm you."

Cecily thought that was a kind thing to say, as though he was more interested in her well-being than in her vermillion-painted mouth or the sapphires sparkling on her fingers. She didn't have the heart to stop him from taking her hand and pressing his lips to her throat. Lying beside his cold body afterward reminded her of sleeping with her sisters before they were only shades. The chill touch of his skin comforted her.

In the morning, the whole house wept with his sudden death. Alice and Mirabelle wept, too, because although he was dead, he did not live on as they did. They could not catch his spirit as he passed.

Cecily rode in a fast coach with her father, and Liam was dead before word reached his household of Vance's burial. The second boy was much easier than she expected. At this wedding, her name had been Alice. In their bedchamber, he'd barely spoken, only torn off her gown and died. There was no time to steal out to the gardens. No time to bury her sisters.

Cecily's father was so pleased he could barely sit still as they pressed on to the palace. He ate an entire box of sweetmeats, chuckling to himself as he watched the landscape fly by.

He had brought something for her to eat, too: a familiar mix of herbs that she left sitting in their bowl.

"I don't want them," she said. "They make me sick."

"Just eat!" he told her. "For once, just do as you are bidden."

She thought about throwing the bowl out of the window and scattering the herbs, but the smell of them reminded her of Mirabelle and Alice, who barely smelled like anything now. Besides, there was nothing else. Cecily ate the herbs.

She could still taste them in her mouth when the carriage arrived at the palace. She half expected to be clapped in irons, and as she passed whispering courtiers, Cecily thought that each one was telling the other a list of her evil deeds.

We first met in the library. I was tall and plain, with pockmarked skin. Yes, I'm the prince in this story. Did you guess, Paul? Cecily later told me that when I first smiled at her, I still appeared to be frowning. What I remember was that she had the blackest eyes I had ever seen.

"This is your betrothed, Cecily," Cecily's father told me.

"I know who she is," I said. She looked very like the picture I had been given. Most girls don't. Your mother certainly didn't.

That afternoon, Cecily washed the dirt of the road off her clothing and went to walk in the gardens of the palace while her father made the final arrangements. The gardens were lush and lovely, more beautiful, even, than those of her father. Plants with heads full of seeds, large as the skulls of infants, lolled from thick stems. She touched the vivid purple and red fronds of one, and it seemed to twitch under her fingers. The lacy foliage of another seemed like the parsley plant of her salad. Crushing it produced a pungent, familiar scent. It was like the breath of her sisters. She bent low for a taste.

"Stop! That's poisonous!" A gardener jogged down the path, wearing steel and leather gloves like those that belonged to her father. His hair flopped over his eyes and he brushed it back impatiently. "You're not supposed to be in this part of the garden."

"I'm sorry," Cecily stammered. "But what are these? I have them in my garden at home."

He snorted. "That isn't very likely. They're hybrids. There are no others like them in all the world."

She thought of the woman at her wedding telling her how her father had once been close to the king. He must have taken cuttings from these very plants.

She began walking, hoping she might leave the gardener behind and be about her burying business. He seemed to misconstrue her wishes, however, pacing alongside her and pointing out prize blooms. She finally managed to put off a lengthy explanation of why the royal apples were the sweetest in the world by pretending a chill and retreating into the palace.

That night there was a feast in Cecily's honor. She sat at a long table set with crisp linens and covered with dishes she was unfamiliar with. There was eel with savory; tiny birds stuffed with berries and herbs, their bones crunching between Cecily's teeth; pears stuffed into almond tarts and soaked in wine; even a sugarcoated pastry in the shape of the palace itself, studded with flecks of gold.

"Oh," Mirabelle gasped. "It is all so lovely."

But Cecily realized that no matter how lovely, it disgusted her to bring the food to her mouth. She looked across the table and saw her father in deep conversation with the king, not at all behaving as if he were out of favor.

That night, Cecily left her room and went out to the garden. Her walk with the gardener had revealed where he kept his tools, and she stole a spade. With her sisters fluttering around her, Cecily looked for the right spot for them to rest. In the moonlight, all the plants were the same, their glossy leaves merely silvery and their flowers shut tight as gates.

"Be careful," Mirabelle said. "You're the only one of us left."

"Whose fault is that?" Cecily demanded.

Neither of them said anything more as Cecily finally chose a place and began to dig. The rich soil parted easily.

That was what I saw her doing as I walked out of the palace. I had been looking for her, but when I found her, digging in the dirt, I didn't know what to say.

She saw me standing there and crouched. Her fingers were black with earth, and she looked feral in the dim light of the palace windows. I don't think she knew it, but I was afraid.

"Please," Cecily said, "I have to finish. I am digging a grave for my sisters."

I thought she was mad then, I admit it. I turned to go back to the house and get the guards, thinking that my plans were in shambles.

"Please," she said again. "I will tell you a secret."

"That you have come to kill me?" I asked her. "As you killed Vance and Liam?"

She frowned.

It was then that I told her the part of her story she did not know and she told most of what I have said tonight.

I will summarize for you, Paul. I know how tedious you find this sort of thing.

When he was a prince like yourself, my father had hired hers to kill those before him in line to the throne. Her father was very efficient; no one doubted but they had merely fallen ill. Mother told me this much before her death, and I told it to Cecily.

Apparently, it was my birth that made Father send Cecily's father to the country. It made him uncomfortable to look at his own son and to consider the sort of son he had once been.

As I got older, however, he grew increasingly certain that I was planning his death. He wrote to Cecily's father and coaxed him from retirement. Her father had a price, of course—Liam and Vance—some grudge avenged. I have forgotten the details. It doesn't matter. Our engagements were arranged.

"How did you find out?" Cecily asked when I finished speaking.

"My mother taught me to go through Father's correspondence." I had not expected her to be both the poison and the poisoner, and I found myself studying her pale skin and black eyes for some sign that it was true. I leaned toward her unconsciously and something about her smell, sweet as rot, made me dizzy. I stepped back abruptly.

"I will make this bargain with you," I said. It was not the bargain I had planned to make, but I tried to speak with confidence. "Kill my father and yours and you may bury your sisters in this garden. I will keep them safe for as long as I shall reign and I shall make a proclamation so that the garden remains the same when I am no more."

She looked at me, and I couldn't tell what she was seeing. "Will you bury me here as well?"

I stammered, trying to come up with an answer. She was smarter than I had given her credit for. Of course she would be caught and slain. Men were coming now from the baronies, I was sure, to avenge the murders of her two husbands.

"I will," I said.

She smiled shyly, but her eyes shone. "And will you tend my grave and the graves of my sisters? Will you bring us flowers and tell us stories?"

I said I would.

Cecily finished the graves for Mirabelle and for Alice. Each girl curled up at the bottom of her pit like pale sworls of fog, and Cecily buried them with her hands.

I wished that she was a normal girl, that I might have taken her hand or pulled her to me to comfort her, but instead I left the garden, chased by my own cowardice.

The next day, she put on her wedding gown and long white gloves and dressed her own hair. At the wedding, she was called Cecily, and she promised to be my good and faithful wife. And she was. The best and most faithful of all my wives.

There was a feast with many toasts, one after the next. The king's face was red with drinking and laughter, but he would not look at me, even when he drank to my health. As a dish of almond tarts was passed, Cecily rose and lifted her own glass. She walked to where her father and the king sat together.

"I want to toast," she said, and the assembled company fell silent. It was not the normal way of things for a bride to speak. She pulled off those gloves as we watched.

"I would thank my father, who made me, and the king, who also had a hand in my making." With those words, she leaned down and took her father's face in her hands and pressed her lips to his. He struggled, but her grip was surprisingly firm. I wondered what her mouth felt like.

"Farewell, Father," she said. He fell back upon his chair, choking. She laughed, not with mirth or even mockery, but something that was closer to a sob. "You crafted me so sharp, I cut even myself."

The king looked puzzled as she turned and took his hand in hers. He must have been very drunk, now that he thought himself safe from me. Certainly he wore no gloves. He pulled his fingers free with such force that he knocked over his wine. The pinkish tide spread across the white tablecloth as he died.

They shot her, of course. The guards. Eventually even she fell. ▧

Yes, I suppose I embellished the story in places and perhaps I was a little dramatic, but that hardly matters.

What does matter is that after they shot her, I had her carried out to the garden—carefully, ever so carefully—and buried beside her sisters.

From each grave bloomed a plant covered in thorns, with petals like velvet. Its flowers are quite poisonous, too, but you already know that. Yes, the very plant you tried to poison me with. I knew its scent well—acrid and heavy—too well not to notice it in this golden cup you gave me, even mixed with cider.

In a few minutes the servants will come and unbind you. Surprised? Ah, well, a father ought to have a few surprises for his only son. You will make a fine king, Paul. And for myself, I will take this beautiful goblet, bring it to my lips, and drink. Talking as much as I have makes one thirsty.

I have left instructions as to where I would like to be buried. No, not near your mother, as much as I was occasionally fond of her. Beside the flowers in the west garden. You know the ones.

Perhaps I should take the gag from your mouth so that you might protest your innocence, exclaim your disbelief, tell your father good-bye. But I do not think I will. I find I rather appreciate the silence.

Honey in the Wound

Nancy Etchemendy

For the better part of my life, I have borne the circumstances of Avery Channing's death in silence, at first because I wished to forget them, later because I doubted anyone would believe the truth, and later still because I feared I might suffer eternal damnation for my part in the whole terrible business. But time has worked a certain alchemy. I have no greater wish than to die with a clear conscience, and the prospect of confessing seems less awful now than it once did. I was only a child. When that is considered, what I did seems easier to understand.

I was ten years old when, on the afternoon of November 13, 1925, we heard a shuffling on the porch, followed by a scream and whimpers. I was in the kitchen at the time, arguing with my mother about Lon Chaney's new movie, *The Phantom of the Opera*, which was showing

at the cinema down the street. Mother said it was hideous trash, and no, I could not go see it. The house was
warm and smelled of apple pie. There was a window over
the sink, and the reds, oranges, and yellows of the leaves
outside were so vibrant that they flowed into the room,
permeating it with surreal color.

"What on earth was that?" said Mother, and hurried
toward the parlor, drying her hands on her apron. She
threw the front door open, never pausing to look through
the glass. The things we feared—wars and sickness and
grief—could not be kept out by doors or locks, anyway.

Before us stood a clump of sweaty boys. There were
four at the bottom of the steps and three on the porch—
Charlie Boynton, Will Lowder, and between them, their
friend, my brother Avery. All of them were scratched and
streaked with mud. That wasn't so unusual. They were
twelve and thirteen years old, and boys play rough. The
unusual thing was the silence. No jostling, no laughter.
Just the whisper of frantic breath.

"We . . . we were only playing," said Charlie. "It
wasn't anybody's fault." His face was tight with the effort it took not to cry.

Only then did I notice that Charlie and Will had their
arms under Avery in a fireman's carry. His hair hung over
his eyes in dark, wet strings. His skin looked pale as bone.
He was shivering, and grunting with pain. Blood soaked
his right pant leg, drip-drip-dripping onto the gray-painted
boards in a crimson pool the size of a dinner plate.

Mother, it must now be said, knew what it was like to lose a child. My brother George, three years older than Avery, had died in the influenza pandemic at the age of nine. I was very small at the time. I didn't remember much about him. But I did recall Mother's eyes on the day of his death. Their emptiness had terrified me, as had the stillness of her hands when I tried to make them hold me.

She had the same look about her now, as if she were slipping toward the edge of the earth, beyond which lay a great and nameless abyss. A lone crow yawped from the branches of the chestnut tree across the street. A gust of wind rattled the leaves, bringing with it the scent of fear.

"Mama!" I cried, grabbing at her dress.

But Avery wasn't dead yet, might still be saved, and he needed her more than I did. She helped the boys lay him down on the porch, where the brightening red puddle spread around him.

"Hester, go get your father! Tell him to bring his bag," she said, her voice so twisted with dread that I only knew it was hers by watching her lips.

"Yes, ma'am," I said, glad to turn away and run from Avery's bone face and Mother's eyes and the blood.

Gumtree was a much smaller town in those days than it is now. There weren't but a few thousand people in all of Hamilton County, and most of those lived fifty miles north of us in Ferrensburg, which we thought of as "the city." My father was Gumtree's only doctor—a lucky thing, you'll say. Perhaps. Perhaps not. If he had been a grocer or a haberdasher, I do not think the horror would have come to pass. Avery would simply have died, and very probably it would have happened right there on the porch.

As it was, I changed the natural course of things by making a headlong dash through the house and down the back steps to the small, separate cottage where my father saw his patients. I found him listening, probably in vain, to the black and shriveled heart of Thomas Thatcher, the owner of Gumtree Bank and Trust, whose flabby, hairy chest I remember to this day.

I tried to tell Father what had happened, but all that came out of my mouth was a mishmash of nonsense. It would have been easier for me to sprout wings and fly to New Orleans than it was to tell him to bring his bag. But I suppose my face must have told the story, for he took one look, snatched up his black satchel, and tore after me as I headed back toward the porch, leaving Mr. Thatcher all asputter.

Father had spent time on the Western Front in the Great War, something Mother hadn't yet forgiven him for. At age thirty-two, he'd been too old for the draft. He didn't have to go. He volunteered. When George died, Father was four thousand miles away in a hospital tent in Arleux, tending someone else's son. The war taught him many things, but perhaps the most important was the value of his own children. The next most important was what to do with a leg that looked like Avery's.

With a practiced hand, Father applied a tourniquet. He and the boys carried Avery around to the cottage, where Mr. Thatcher, still buttoning his shirt, beat a hasty retreat. There they stretched my brother out in the surgery and tied him down while Father sterilized his instruments and scrubbed his hands. Mother scrubbed hers as well, for he had trained her to assist him with such cases, and like it or not, there was no one else who knew how to help.

The boys and I were sent out to wait in the little anteroom. There we sat in misery as the fearsome smell of ether drifted out from under the door. While the first hour passed, they told me the story in whispered gasps, their voices rising now and then in spite of them.

They had been playing, it turned out, in the Redfield house, long abandoned, boarded up, and condemned. On a dare, Avery had crept up the broken, sagging stairs to the second story, where—it was rumored—the glowing ghost of old Mr. Redfield had occasionally been seen peering out a window. There in the shadowy master bedroom Avery was startled, not by a ghost, but by a large rat that ran out from under the bed. No doubt it had lived unmolested for years in the stuffing of the rotten mattress and was as electrified by the sight of Avery as Avery was by the flash of something horrid and alive festooned in cobwebs.

He jumped backward, landing hard and off-balance on the termite-ridden floor. I have pictured the scene too many times to count—the boards giving way with a splintering crack, his hands scrabbling at wood that came away in them, his scream as he crashed down into the parlor, a milky dust of vermin smut rising around him, bats fluttering from their roosts in the corners of the high ceiling. And above all, how it must have felt when the bone of his leg split and came up like a knife through the muscles and tendons, puncturing the artery.

One by one the boys left to go home to dinners that went largely uneaten. By dusk there was no one left but me. I thought of walking up to the house for some bread and cheese or an apple, but after all that I had seen and heard, monsters lurked in every shadow. So I sat rigid on a hard white-painted chair listening to the rumble of my stomach and the wind in the trees till fear of the dark overcame my fear of moving, and I got up and lit a lamp.

I do not know what time it was when Father carried me to bed. He and our neighbor, Mr. Hoskins, had already moved Avery on a stretcher to a downstairs room in the house, near enough to the kitchen so he could be easily nursed. By then the artery and the wound had been cleaned and stitched closed, the bone set, and a plaster cast applied. And Avery had received a pint of Father's blood topped off with an injection of morphine. Still his

groans echoed up the stairwell all night long as if from
hell itself.

Demons walked my dreams. I woke shivering a number of times. But no one came when I called out. Avery
needed our parents more than I. It was to be the unspoken rule for some time to come.

Avery's recovery went well at first. Within twenty-four
hours he was able to eat a little clear broth, and within
forty-eight, Charlie and Will were allowed to come for a
brief visit. Within sixty hours, I was pressed into service
reading pulp westerns and playing endless games of check-
ers with the invalid to keep his mind off the pain. And
within seventy-two, Avery had homework from the inim-
itable Miss Miller, and he and I were quarreling energet-
ically in the usual way. Things were going beautifully.

Then one evening he developed a fever. Father had
left a hole in the cast so air could get to the wound where
the bone had broken the skin, and by the next morning,
brownish, foul-smelling pus bubbled from it. Our patient lay tossing and turning in sheets soaked with sweat.
I thought of the Redfield house—the poisoned snow of
dust laden with rat filth and dry rot sifting down over
Avery's opened skin.

Just an infection, you'll say. Nothing a ten-day course
of antibiotics couldn't cure. But in 1925, antibiotics had
not yet been discovered. We were still relying on carbolic

acid, scalpels, bone saws, and hope in cases like Avery's. The word *infection* struck the same fear in the belly then as *cancer* does now.

Father had to remove the cast and clean the wound with carbolic while Mother and I did our best to hold Avery still. Even after a dose of morphine and a shot of bourbon whiskey, he thrashed and screamed. I held my eyes closed tight and prayed to be forgiven for quarreling with him, and I prayed he wouldn't die—prayed so hard that for a time the rest of the world receded.

Someone called my name. The first time, I heard it as if in a dream; the second time more clearly; and the third time, as my shoulders were shaken by strong hands, I opened my eyes.

It was Mother. She pressed a quarter into my hand. "Run to Mr. Ursari's," she said. "Bring back a honeycomb. Hurry!"

"Yes, ma'am," I replied, and made a dash for the front door, leaping high over the place where Avery's blood had pooled when they brought him home, traces of which remained.

A bank of clouds had rolled in from the north, and a cold wind moaned through the trees. I'd forgotten my coat. Goose bumps rose on my skin. Still, I ran and did not turn back. Petrus Ursari's place wasn't far, just down the street and around the corner at the edge of town. He lived alone in a tiny house—little more than a shack, really—on three acres of land dotted with beehives, chicken coops, and peach trees.

I didn't know him very well, though I felt as if I did, for my friends and I had spent many hours trying to imagine a history that might explain what had brought him to our town and why he stayed. Though the house was small, it was tidy, and painted bright unlikely colors— reds and yellows and blues—irresistible to children. Flattened spoons and bits of glass hung from the eves so that every passing breeze made music from them. Mr. Ursari himself wore a braided beard, which hid the chestnut brown of his face, and a leather vest incised with vines and flowers the same colors as his house. He didn't speak much, and when he did, his words were so heavily accented it was hard to make head or tail of them. His eyes lay like dark eggs in nests of wrinkles, though there was no sign of gray in his jet-black hair. As far as we could tell, there was no Mrs. Ursari or any sons or daughters, nor had there ever been. But because of his taciturn nature, no one knew for sure.

People in Gumtree returned the favor by not having much to do with him. Mother said he wasn't "our kind." Yet he stayed. And everyone bought his eggs, peaches, and honey, for they were famous far and wide for their flavor.

You might think it odd for Mother to send me after honey while my brother lay on what she feared might be his deathbed. Yet it made perfect sense at that time and in that place. The year Mr. Ursari came to Gumtree, Tom Mumford, a local farmer, sliced his leg with an ax. Father treated the wound in the usual way, but in spite of his best efforts, an infection developed and spread. It looked as if Mumford would lose his leg. On the morning of the planned surgery, Father arrived with his tools sharpened and sterilized only to find the infection gone and Mumford seated in bed dining on ham and grits.

According to Mrs. Mumford, Petrus Ursari had stopped by the previous evening with a special piece of honeycomb and instructions to pour some of the honey into the wound and give the rest to Mr. Mumford by mouth. A miracle cure, said the wife. Father pooh-poohed this, saying it was more likely the carbolic acid and blind luck had healed the wound. He'd seen the spontaneous disappearance of infections in the war, not often, but enough to know it sometimes happens.

The fact remained that Mumford's leg was saved, apparently by gypsy honey, and the story traveled like wildfire. After that, as much of Mr. Ursari's honey was used on cuts and scrapes as was used on griddle cakes. Not in our house, however, where Father denounced the practice as ignorant and harmful and lumped it in the same general category with the Scopes trial—a sorry illustration, he said, of how little respect his countrymen had for science and reason.

When I arrived at Mr. Ursari's door, I pounded on it with both fists and called his name. But I got no answer. I opened it a crack and called again. Still no answer, so I stepped inside. The house was warm. Something savory simmered in a kettle on a small woodstove. A coppery beam of sunlight found its way through a break in the clouds to spill across a simple table cluttered with bread and green apples. I could not see a single square inch of wall space that wasn't occupied by some object. Pots and pans hung everywhere—crucifixes, a violin, dried herbs in tied bundles, a mummified frog, a photograph.

I stepped closer. The picture showed a family— mother, father, and three children, one a babe in the mother's arms. They had the stiff look of people dressed in clothes they didn't wear often, intricate with embroidery and starched lace. The man was Mr. Ursari. Tucked under his arm was the violin. Who were they, I wondered, those others? And why were they not here with him now?

Not far from the picture stood a shelf that ran from floor to ceiling. Jars of golden honey were ranked upon it, glowing in the slanted sunlight, each one labeled in careful but indecipherable script. Some of the jars had beeswax combs in them. Others did not.

I was about to pick one, trusting to Providence, and leave the quarter on the table when someone behind me said, "Good day. May I be of service?" I knew before I turned around that it was Mr. Ursari. His voice was unmistakable—foreign, musical, tinged with the same sorrow as his eyes.

"Oh, Mr. Ursari! Thank goodness," I said. "I need some honey for Avery. I'm in the awfulest rush."

"Ah, yes, of course," said Ursari, as if he already knew the whole story, and perhaps he did. In the town of Gumtree, we all knew one another's business. It's just that I couldn't recall any visitors that day who might have carried news of Avery's condition abroad.

He reached a jar from the shelf, not the one I would have taken, and knelt to fold my hands around it.

"It is made from the nectar of lilies in a place known only to my bees. This is the last jar. I pray it is powerful enough. But"—he held me in a gaze that pierced my heart, his face lined with some unspoken burden—"know that if God wants him, it is best not to stand in the way."

"Thank you. Thank you so much. I have a quarter."

"Keep it," replied Ursari. "Did you understand what I said?"

I nodded, though in fact his warning made very little impression on me at the time. "Thank you. I have to get home."

"Of course."

I turned, back through the door and down the worn stairs, torn by a desire to hurry and the need to be careful of the treasure I cradled in my cold, skinny arms—

the last jar of lily honey from a place known only to bees, and the last remnant of hope for my brother.

Somehow the jar made it home in one piece. My mother whisked it from my hands and administered the first of it to Avery the minute my father's back was turned. When Father discovered what she'd done, he literally pulled his hair. He shouted at her till she shrank into a corner in tears. The honey wasn't sterile, he said. It would just make Avery sicker, and she had done a stupid, stupid thing. In his rage, he went so far as to ask her if she wanted their only remaining son to die. Then he went to the cottage, got his instruments, and prepared to amputate Avery's leg.

I hid in my room and sobbed. I did not want Avery to be crippled, nor did I want to be an only child. Neither did I want to think that I had made things worse by going to Mr. Ursari's. Having been held in Ursari's dark, sad gaze, I knew he truly thought the honey might cure Avery. A great confusion descended on my young mind, for I had hitherto thought of all adults as fonts of wisdom. Yet there was the wise, good man Ursari giving me honey, and there was the wise, good man my father raging at how wrong that was. Where had the truth gone? This I wondered often in the coming hours.

I must have slept awhile, for it was sunset when I awoke. Cherry-red clouds swirled across the sky. I cracked the door and listened for some sound—a laugh, a moan, a sob—that might tell me what it was for which I must now prepare myself. Someone was singing. Very softly.

I crept down the stairs, my heart flinging itself against my ribs as if they were a cage. For beneath the scents of cut roses in the entryway, the broth on the stove, the tart leather of Father's favorite chair, and every other smell in the house, the stink of rotting meat lay like the low drone of flies.

When I peeked around the corner into Avery's sickroom, I could not at first make sense of what I saw. His eyes, ordinarily gas-flame blue, were cloudy gray, staring fixedly at nothing. An ether mask lay on his pillow like some forgotten toy. Father's instruments, spattered crimson, sat in a tray on a side table. Avery's leg lay on the bed beside him. Below the scraped knee, it looked powdery and pale as an egg. Above, it looked like spoiled fruit. I say the leg lay beside him advisedly, for that is the literal truth. Father had succeeded in amputating it. But then something had happened—something that made him tear the ether mask from Avery's face, forget to clean his tools, and leave a surgically severed limb in plain sight dripping on the patient's blanket. Avery had died.

Obvious though it was, Mother did not appear to believe it. My brother's jaw had stiffened in death, but still she spooned honey into his mouth, wrenching his teeth apart to do it. "When you wake, you'll have cake, and all the pretty little horses," she crooned.

"Mama, what are you doing?" I said.

She looked up, surprise fluttering across her face. "Why, Hester, it's you. What kind of question is that? Can't you see I'm"—she tilted her head and frowned at Avery, then at the spoon in her hand—"I'm giving your brother his medicine."

Cold tentacles wrapped themselves around my heart, threatening to stop it. My knees wobbled. "Where is Father?" I asked.

"I don't know where he's gone," she replied. "Perhaps to see a patient." She dipped the spoon into the honey jar. "I wonder, could you get me a cup of tea? I can't leave Avery just now."

I stared hard at the corpse, uncertain what to do. What made her think he was still alive? I leaned closer.

With a jerk, Avery's arm rose two inches off the bed, and an inhuman groan issued from his mouth along with a stink too horrid to describe.

I squealed and jumped back so fast and hard that I hit the opposite wall, where I cringed, gripped as if by ague.

Mother calmly reached out and pushed the arm back down onto the bed. "Yes, Avery, it's Sister," she said. "She's come to see how you are."

Avery moaned again.

Only then did it dawn on me that he was saying my name, or trying to.

"Hester, what's the matter with you? Go get the tea, please," said Mother, and held the spoon to her son's gray lips. Honey ran down his chin in yellow rivulets, pooling in the hollow of his throat.

Picking myself up, I gladly ran for the kitchen.

There I set about stoking the stove and checking the water in the kettle, trying hard to do the job Mother had given me and to think about nothing else. Still, my teeth chattered, and it was not from the cold. I was shaking Darjeeling into the blue china pot when the sound of heavy footsteps on the stairs outside froze me in place. I could not turn to peer through the black glass panes of the door. I could not so much as squeak.

"Hester?" It was Father.

I threw down the tea tin and tried to fling my arms around him. But instead of the familiar smell of his soap and the soft wool of his coat and trousers, my face met with hard, gouging corners. His arms were full of books. His hair, which he generally kept neat to a fault, stuck out at odd angles. His eyes were wide and red-rimmed. I took a step backward without meaning to.

"Something's wrong with Avery," I said.

"Yes, I know," he replied. "You're making tea?"

I nodded.

"Would you bring me a cup? I'll be with Mother." He moved toward the doorway.

I touched his coat sleeve. "Is he dead?"

He looked at me, the deep lines between his eyes growing deeper still, his nostrils large and dark, the corners of his handsome mouth drooping.

"I don't know," he said, and brushed past me with his burden.

When the tea was ready, I loaded a tray and carried it to the sickroom. Mother had fallen asleep in the rocking chair. The honey jar gleamed at her elbow, half empty. Father hunched on the edge of the bed with two books open on his lap and the others stacked at his feet. Now I could see their titles, gleaming gold on the good leather spines: *Humphrey's Remedies. Nature of Living Organisms. The Merck Manual.* I poured him a cup of tea and set it in a saucer on the topmost book, *Horner's Physiology of Death.*

The leg still lay on the bed. I saw quite suddenly that in all that sea of terrors it was the one problem I had the power to solve. That leg had carried me pig-a-back, walked me home from school, run from me in games of hide-and-seek, and climbed the stairs of the Redfield house to seal Avery's fate. It ought to be treated better than some forgotten piece of meat.

So while Father sought his answers in the written works of rational men, I took an old sheet from the linen cupboard and carefully wrapped the errant limb. I do not know how much a human leg weighs. Avery was not full grown, and what I carried was not his entire leg, some portion of which was still attached to his body. Nevertheless, it was heavy. It took me quite some time just to get my strange parcel out to the garden, and longer still to locate a shovel. The hardest part of all was the digging, which I chose to do in Mother's rose bed because I knew the soil was soft there. All of this took place by the light of a lantern in a brisk wind.

When I had finished, I removed my muddy shoes, came back into the house, and washed my hands in the kitchen sink. The exertion had done me good. The shivering had stopped, and my mind was clearer. I went straight to the sickroom to see what Father had found out.

The books lay scattered across the floor. A few were open, facedown, the beloved spines cracked.

"Father?" I whispered. But he didn't answer. He was far too busy spooning honey into Avery's mouth and onto the open stump of his leg.

By the light of the coal oil lamp, I could see that Avery's muscles had begun to relax a little. His eyes, deep in the sockets of his skull, were closed. His lips had slightly parted to reveal his strong white teeth, which I had long envied. His pallid skin lay draped over the bones of his face like a sheet of melted wax.

"Father?" I said again, a little louder. Still he did not respond. His arm moved again and again, spooning the honey.

I crept up close enough to touch Avery's hand. It was cold as snow. It did not move, nor did any other part of him—no rise or fall of lungs, no flutter of veins, no whisper of breath.

Surely I had imagined his crying my name, or merely wished it.

It was as if something broke loose inside me then. I put my hands on Father's shoulders and tried with all my child's might to shake him. I meant to speak in a normal way, but the words would not be spoken. They had to be screamed. "Stop it! Can't you see he's dead? Stop!"

At last Father responded. "No, he's not."

"He is, he is!" I cried.

That is when Avery's eyelids flew open to reveal the shrunken gray orbs beneath, which he turned on me like beads of ice. As I listened in horror, the effigy of a song began to issue from him. "Way down yonder in the meadow, there's a poor wee little lamby."

I hesitate to say that he was singing, for it wasn't a human voice. Rather it was a rattle that forced its way up through bubbles of honey. "Birds and butterflies pickin' at its eyes, crying for its mammy," he went on—the second verse of Mother's lullaby.

At which point, words abandoned me entirely, and I ran screaming up the stairs to my room, where I bolted the door and jammed a chair against it.

After I had lit the lamp, I pushed my bed into the corner of the room farthest from the door, climbed into it fully clothed, and pulled the covers over my head. I couldn't stop shaking, and I couldn't seem to catch my breath. The worst of it was that my parents frightened me just as much as poor, ruined Avery. My child's mind parsed the situation out this way: either they had taken leave of their senses, in which case I was at the mercy of lunatics, or I had taken leave of my own and would be sent to an asylum as soon as someone noticed.

Like a dog with a bone stuck in its teeth, I worried the question of what to do, turning and twisting in the dark shelter of the blanket, wetting my pillowcase and my beloved rag doll with tears. I could go find a neighbor— Mr. Hoskins, or Will or Charlie's mother perhaps—and place myself in their hands. But if I turned out to be the crazy one, this would only hasten my exile to bedlam. I could run away. I had a small suitcase. There were hunks of bacon and some potatoes in the pantry that I could take with me to eat. Maybe I could hop a train. But Mother said never to hang about by the tracks, for bad men some-times idled there, waiting to make trouble for unwary little girls. And besides, there was no moon. The branch of a tree outside my window scritch-scratched against the glass like the bone of an amputated leg.

I do not know how many hours passed, for there was no clock in my room. I do not think I slept, lit up as I was with the peculiar energy of hysteria. I can only say that the lamp was still burning when I poked my head out from beneath the covers.

There was a sound on the stairs. Not an ordinary sound like Father's footsteps or a mouse. No. This was a sound like the dragging of a gunny sack filled with things both hard and soft, *slither, thud, slither, thud,* coming closer and closer to my room. Something scratched at the door. Then the doorknob rattled. I could not help but look. I saw the knob turn.

"Hester, Hester." It was the bubbling, honeyed voice of Avery's corpse.

"Get away!" I screamed.

"Jesus, help me. Please." This was followed by a heavy thump and a pitiful scrabbling against the wood. I pictured Avery there, having dragged himself up the stairs on his elbows because he had only one leg. Blind. Doing everything by feel, or by following the scent of his sister.

I felt as if a heavy board with rocks upon it lay over my heart. My breath came in gasps. I could not imagine how I might help him. I could think only of how I might help myself. Knock him down the stairs? He would just come back up. Cut off his head? It would probably still implore me.

It was then that Mr. Ursari's words came back to me. *Know that if God wants him, it is best not to stand in the way.* Quite suddenly, I knew what I must do. I leaped out of bed, grabbed my coat from the hook in the closet. I would not brave what lay beyond my door. I climbed out the window instead, hiking up my skirt to shinny down the trellis that, in softer seasons, supported the large violet blossoms of Mother's clematis. Thence I ran through the moonless streets to the house of Petrus

Ursari and pounded on his door with both my fists, shrieking like a child banshee and weeping.

Lamplight flared in the window, the door opened, and
there he stood, barefoot, lace-trimmed nightshirt stuffed
into his trousers, his sad face creased and cloudy with
sleep. "Child, what is wrong?" he said, and shepherded
me into his dim abode.

Soon I was seated beside the stove, my hands wrapped
around a cup of hot cider, telling him the whole miser-
able tale.

When I was finished, he said, "Ones you love, it is
hard to let go."

I knew somehow by the way he said it that he had
done more than his fair share of letting go.

"Was it them?" I said, looking toward the photograph
of the woman and children. "Were they who you had to
let go?"

He nodded, gazing not at me but at them, or through
them, to the faraway land where they all had once lived
together. Without rising, he reached up and took a small
blue bottle from the shelf. He set it on the table before
me. It was square, like a medicine bottle, and corked.
The wax seal was broken. Whatever the bottle contained,
it had been used at least once before.

"What is it?" I asked.

"A liqueur, made from many things, living and dead."

I was afraid to ask what those things might be.
Mummified peaches from trees in graveyards? Mashed

eyeballs? Toad claws? The water from some haunted stream in the Carpathian Mountains? But those abominations could hold no candle to what came next.

"You must rub it on his heart," said Mr. Ursari.

I pressed my hand against the place under which I thought my own heart must lie. "Here, you mean?"

But he shook his head, and the lines of sorrow in his face deepened. "The heart itself."

I squinted at him, trying hard to find some subtle and harmless meaning in those awful words, but there was none.

"Y . . . you don't mean . . ." I stuttered.

He leaned forward, placed his palms upon the table, and held me in that powerful gaze of his. "The heart itself," he repeated. "Tell no one. I am sorry. There is no other way."

That is how I came to stand at the top of our stairs at sunrise on a November day, a kitchen knife in one hand and a small blue bottle in my pocket. Avery lay on his side, still as a winter-killed hare, his cheek pressed against the thin carpet. I suppose they had taken off his clothes before the surgery, for he was naked. There were big purple splotches on his back, which I later learned were probably from pooled blood. The stump of his leg was still unbandaged and unclosed, sticky with honey. It stank like the bin behind the butcher shop on a hot day.

"Avery?" I whispered.

He did not move. My spirits leaped at the possibility that perhaps he was truly dead after all.

I called again. "Avery?" praying he wouldn't answer. There was no response.

"Oh," I sobbed, and went down on my knees in a paroxysm of pain and gratitude, the knife forgotten.

Imagine the purity of my horror when he rolled onto his back and a long, anguished groan escaped his throat. I scuttled backward, my own vocal cords shocked silent. Outside, the first little bit of sun peeped over the horizon. My bedroom door stood open, and through the window came a finger of light. Red as blood, it lay across Avery's dead face, warming it. I swear a tear rolled glimmering down his cheek.

I inched back toward him, my arm stretched out for the knife, and when I got close enough, I seized it. I held it in both hands. I still recall how the hard wood of the handle pressed into my skin. "Hold still," I said, opened my eyes, and did what had to be done.

I will not leave you with the details, which are predictably grim, as my knowledge of anatomy was minimal at the time. There was a good deal of fumbling. I will say that when I applied Ursari's potion as directed, Avery sighed. Even now I still believe a pale, vaporous shape drifted up from him to meet that crimson shaft of sunlight. Before my parents awoke and discovered my handiwork, I went back to Mr. Ursari's and knocked on the door. There was no answer, so I left the blue bottle and its remaining contents on the porch, the cork stuck in as far as it would go.

My father, who was on good terms with the Hamilton County coroner, arranged the legalities in such a way that no questions were ever asked. I became my parents' only child. I wish I could say that the love they once lavished on their sons was thereafter mine and mine alone. But if I am honest, I must admit that even before Avery died, there had stood between my parents and me a wall of something thin and clear and cold as the first ice of winter on a familiar pond. I was not George, who was gone. And I was not Avery, who replaced him.

Whatever the reasons, the ice thickened until I begged to be sent away to school and they obliged. After that I saw them only in the summers. We did not speak of Avery's death except in the most general terms. Nor did we speak of Ursari's honey, which we never tasted again, though Mother purchased his eggs and, in season, his peaches, until he disappeared one day without preamble, his house abandoned, his belongings gone. My brother died of an infected wound, and there is no evidence to the contrary. Except for my own sorrow, that heavy stone I've carried all these years and now gladly lay down before you. May I rest as well as he.

M. T. ANDERSON has published several novels for teens, including *Thirsty; The Game of Sunken Places; Feed;* and *The Astonishing Life of Octavian Nothing, Traitor to the Nation, Volume One: The Pox Party,* which received a National Book Award. "In 'The Gray Boy's Work,'" he says, "I tried to reproduce the stark, severe, simple textures of early American art. At the same time, I wanted to capture the irreducible emotional complexity of this family. That's why the whole time I was trying to write the story, Complete Irritation was squatting on my computer, laughing his ass off."

M. T. Anderson lives in Massachusetts.

HOLLY BLACK is the author of three contemporary fantasy novels, *Tithe: A Modern Faerie Tale,* the Norton Award–winning *Valiant: A Modern Tale of Faerie,* and *Ironside: A Modern Faery's Tale,* as well as the best-selling series the Spiderwick Chronicles. Of "The Poison Eaters," she says, "I was inspired by Hawthorne's 'Rappaccini's Daughter' and by the idea that a sin eater could offer absolution by taking on the sins of another (through sin-soaked bread, but I didn't manage to work that in)."

Holly Black lives in Massachusetts, with her husband, Theo, and often travels to a local coffeehouse to sit near Kelly Link, drink buckets of coffee, and pretend to work.

LIBBA BRAY has experienced lots of scary things, not the least of which include giving herself a home perm in tenth grade and dressing up as the members of Kiss with her best friends for no apparent reason. She is the author of the *New York Times* best-selling novels *A Great and Terrible Beauty* and *Rebel Angels*.

"'Bad Things' was inspired by a real incident," she says. "When I was in high school in North Texas, there were some cow mutilations that took place on the outskirts of town, and the rumors of satanic rituals ran fast and furiously— absolute catnip for a bunch of bored, imaginative sixteen-year-olds. So my friend Les picked us all up in his pickup, and we drove out there to play chicken with the devil worshippers, who never materialized. Mostly, we drank beer, listened to bad metal bands, and talked honestly. And what could be scarier than that?"

Libba Bray lives in New York City, where there are no cows that she knows of.

HERBIE BRENNAN recently celebrated publication of his 104th book, *The Purple Emperor*, a sequel to his *New York Times* bestseller, *Faerie Wars*. A longtime student of sorcery, he discovered an old copy of the *Lemegeton, or the Lesser Key of Solomon* (a book that really does exist) in a junk shop and used it to conjure up "The Necromancers." The magical techniques described in the story are authentic, but cautiously edited to protect the reader.

Herbie Brennan lives in Ireland.

NANCY ETCHEMENDY's fiction for children and adults has appeared regularly for the past twenty-five years, both in the United States and abroad. Her work has earned a number of honors, including three Bram Stoker Awards (two for children's horror). Her most recent novel, science fiction for children, is *The Power of Un*. Her collection of short dark fantasy for young adults, *Cat in Glass and Other Tales of the Unnatural*, was named an American Library Association Best Book for Young Adults.

About "Honey in the Wound," she says, "A peculiar thing happened with this story. I started work on it in March of 2005, at the height of the Terri Schiavo furor. I thought I was just writing a nice, creepy zombie story. But I guess the newspaper articles were on my mind more than I realized. Because, well . . . the similarities are pretty clear. It's not so much about a zombie as it is about being able to die when it's time."

Nancy Etchemendy lives and works in northern California, where she leads a somewhat schizophrenic life, alternating between unkempt, introverted writer of weird tales and requisite gracious wife of Stanford University's provost.

ANNETTE CURTIS KLAUSE was born in Bristol, England. "When I was fifteen," she says, "my family moved to the United States. It was summer. School was out. I didn't know anyone. So my closest friend was my twelve-year-old sister, Julie. I had a much younger sister and a brother would be born a year later, but Julie and I were near in age, so we shared a bedroom, invented elaborate games together, fought, made up, and fought again.

"In America we shared the same friends, though she was in middle school and I was in high school. People thought she was prettier than me, though, and she was outgoing and made friends easily while I was still shy. I was jealous of her for that and proud of her at the same time. She knew my weaknesses and wasn't afraid to hurt me out of spite; she infuriated me frequently, yet we could laugh for hours. But she grew up too fast, she made bad choices, and as she became older she got herself in a whole bunch of trouble, bad trouble. She had her own vampires, but under the turmoil, the crises, the pain, she still had a keen intelligence and an iron will, and she overcame tremendous odds to put her life back together.

"The problem is, sometimes the vampires of your past come back to bite you on the ass. Julie died of liver disease in February 2005, around the same time I was asked for a story for this anthology. I had a title I was eager to use, and I wanted it to be a zombie story, but, let's face it, zombies aren't too sexy—all those body parts falling off—so I kept on coming back to vampires. It wasn't until I started writing the story, however, that I realized it wasn't just about vampires; it was about my feelings for my sister.

"My newest book is called *Freaks: Alive, on the Inside!* I can hear Julie say —'That one's about you, huh?' I'm glad I can still hear her laughter in my head."

Annette Curtis Klause lives in Maryland with her husband and six cats.

KELLY LINK is the author of two collections, *Stranger Things Happen* and *Magic for Beginners*. She co-edits the fantasy half of *The Year's Best Fantasy and Horror* (St. Martin's) with her husband, Gavin J. Grant. Her short stories have won the Tiptree, World Fantasy, and Nebula Awards. She also once won a free trip around the world by answering the question, "Why do you want to go around the world?" ("Because you can't go through it.")

Of "The Wrong Grave," she says, "For several months, I knew I wanted to write a story about a boy who meant to dig up his girlfriend's grave, but instead (somehow) dug up the wrong grave. I started there, and the rest of the story, from the narrator down to the fact that dead people like to eat beef jerky, came as a complete surprise to me.

"I've always been interested in the resurrectionists (people who dug up the recently dead or sometimes just murdered their victims in order to sell their bodies to doctors), as well as the true story, which I mention, about the poet and painter Dante Gabriel Rossetti. As for the wrong dead girl's hair, the folklore about hair that kept growing after someone's death has always seemed terribly creepy. That, and I've been watching far too many Japanese horror movies."

Kelly Link lives in Massachusetts, and she and the writer Holly Black frequently work together at a local coffeehouse that serves watermelon smoothies.

DEBORAH NOYES is the author of a novel, *Angel and Apostle*, and the editor of *Gothic! Ten Original Dark Tales*. Of "No Visible Power," she says, "I'm always riveted by unreliable narrators and wanted to try my hand at creating one of my own. Though the characters in the story are made up, the paranormal events are based on two historic hauntings—one reported in Stratford, Connecticut, in 1850, and another in Windsor, Vermont, in 1955."

Deborah Noyes lives in Massachusetts.

MARCUS SEDGWICK is the author of several books, including *Witch Hill* and *The Book of Dead Days*, both of which were nominated for the Edgar Allan Poe Award. The most recent of these nominations rekindled a fascination with Poe that has borne fruit here in the form of "The Heart of Another"—inspired by Poe's "The Tell-Tale Heart." Of his story, Sedgwick says, "This was one of those stories that I thought might be a novel originally but actually was much better suited to the tight form of the short story. I had the initial idea some years ago but was just waiting for the right ingredient to come along. Poe's story, as well as his own fascination with technique, provided that final piece of the puzzle."

Marcus Sedgwick lives in England.

CHRIS WOODING's first book was accepted for publication when he was nineteen, allowing him to "neatly sidestep the inconvenience of getting a real job." He has been a professional author ever since. Now thirty, he has published more than a dozen books for teens and an epic fantasy sequence for adults, and won several awards for his work. Lately, he has turned his attention to screenwriting and has two films and a cartoon series in development. His gothic horror-fantasy *The Haunting of Alaizabel Cray* was recently published in the United States to great acclaim, followed by his dark anti-fairytale *Poison*.

"'The House and the Locket' is a traditional Victorian ghost story," he says. "I love the tone of that era, the idea of these plummy, eminently sensible people having their stiff upper lips shattered by forces beyond their understanding."

Chris Wooding lives and works in London.

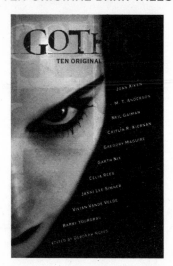

It's sweet to be scared...

A lovesick count and the ghost of his brutalized servant ...
a serial killer who defies death ... a house with a
violent mind of its own. Here are witches who feast
on faces, changeling rites of passage, and a venerable
vampire contemplating his own end.

Ten contemporary writers pay homage to the gothic tale;
it's sweet to be scared, so uncover your eyes, catch your
breath and enter the world of **GOTHIC!**

"Intrepid readers will relish the delicious shivers
– but may want to keep the lights on."
The Horn Book

"Original stories that range from gloomy to
downright terrifying... Brrr."
Kirkus

Can there be any more terrifying tale than this?

Reader, step not lightly into the pages of this book, for herein lies the tale of Count Dracula, lord of the Un-dead, who rises nightly from his coffin to feed on the blood of the living.

Have you the courage to venture into the lunatic asylum, to roam the dark corridors of his castle in Transylvania? Come, come, you must not resist – the children of the night are calling you.

BRAM STOKER'S *Dracula* : RE-EDITED BY JAN NEEDLE FOR THE TWENTY-FIRST CENTURY READER

"Not a book for the faint-hearted! ...The greatest ever vampire story." *Junior Education*